Also by ANN CAMERON

Gloria Rising

Gloria's Way

The Secret Life of Amanda K. Woods

More Stories Huey Tells

The Stories Huey Tells

Julian, Dream Doctor

The Most Beautiful Place in the World

Julian, Secret Agent

Julian's Glorious Summer

More Stories Julian Tells

The Stories Julian Tells

Colibrí

Colibrí

ANN CAMERON

Frances Foster Books

FARRAR STRAUS GIROUX

New York

Copyright © 2003 by Ann Cameron
All rights reserved
Distributed in Canada by Douglas & McIntyre Ltd.
Printed in the United States of America
Designed by Nancy Goldenberg
First edition, 2003
1   3   5   7   9   10   8   6   4   2

Library of Congress Cataloging-in-Publication Data
Cameron, Ann, 1943–
    Colibrí / Ann Cameron.— 1st ed.
        p. cm.
    Summary: Kidnapped when she was very young by an unscrupulous man
who has forced her to lie and beg to get money, a twelve-year-old Mayan
girl endures an abusive life, always wishing she could return to the parents
she can hardly remember.
    ISBN 0-374-31519-1
    [1. Kidnapping—Fiction.   2. Mayas—Fiction.   3. Indians of Central
America—Guatemala—Fiction.   4. Guatemala—Fiction.]   I. Title.

PZ7.C1427 Col 2003
[Fic]—dc21

                                                          2002192542

To Yovany and Jacquelin, *mis nietos*

▲▲▲ CONTENTS ▲▲▲

Colibrí

1

The Valley

Moss and bright grasses glistened around the spring. The earth smelled as if it were singing.

I scooped up water in my hands and drank.

We ate our last pieces of dry bread. I shook the crumbs out of my shawl, folded it into a square, and put it on my head to shade my eyes.

"Let's go, Rosa," Uncle said.

He always called me Rosa. My real name, Tzunún, was a secret I had almost forgotten.

The road was narrow. We walked on, Uncle carrying our belongings on his back in the black suitcase with the broken zipper. So nothing would fall out, he'd stuffed the suitcase inside a rope bag with a carrying strap. The leather strap went around his forehead and left a mark there.

We were in the Ixil Valley, in the high mountains of Guatemala where it rains a lot and sometimes there's frost in the winter. Beside us was a forest of tall pines with flowers in the sunlit spaces—tiny star-shaped red ones, shaggy purple ones with rough raggedy leaves, and seven-foot-tall yellow daisies. The daisies were my favorite, the way they bent their heads and seemed to smile at me.

There were rocks all around, too—enormous boulders that had tumbled down the mountains in ancient times and got to flatter land and just hit a place where they stuck.

Pinecone seeds sprouted on top of boulders, driving their roots into the rock. They'd cracked some boulders wide open.

The seeds in pinecones are lighter than a grain of sand. Sometimes I'd held them in my hand and blown them away, as if they were fine grains of dust. Yet they had the power deep inside them to split rock. Power silent and invisible, but real as the mountains. What was it? Where did it come from?

I wanted to ask Uncle, but I didn't. He disliked questions. Sometimes for whole days he hardly talked.

Uncle said he was a ladino. That is, he claimed he had some Spanish ancestors way back, as well as Mayan ones—and he said that made him moody and gave him a blood disease. He said his Spanish blood hated his Mayan blood, and his Mayan blood hated his Spanish blood, and they were together in him fighting all the time.

I didn't see how that could be. Blood is blood.

We walked along by pastures where sheep were grazing—white ones and black ones, grown ones and little lambs just learning to walk. I thought they were sweet, but I kept that to myself. Uncle called the people he didn't like—which was most people—"stinking sheep." I figured that meant he didn't like sheep.

Behind us a pickup tore up the road, the grinding of its motor eating the stillness of the forest. We moved out of the way and it rocked along beside us, drowning the smell of grass and pines in smoke. The driver glanced at us, slowing down to see if we wanted a ride. A lot of passengers were already in the back, holding on tight to an iron frame welded to the pickup bed, but there would have been room for us.

Uncle waved the driver on.

That was one of the hard parts of being with Uncle. I could never tell what he would do. Often he would accept a ride, and at the end, when the driver was collecting money from everybody, he would try to sneak away without paying. Other times, even if he had money, he'd turn a ride down and just keep walking as if he could walk to the end of the world.

He was a fast walker. When I was little and couldn't keep up, he used to get mad and say he would give me away.

My sandals were tight and hurt my feet. I was growing fast. Too fast, Uncle said.

I didn't know exactly how old I was, because I had lost track. Uncle figured I was twelve.

We kept walking, and pretty soon we were standing on a ridge, looking down into a valley where a town was spread out like the flat bottom of a bowl. We could see tile and tin roofs of houses, and a big white church in the center of town.

"Nebaj," Uncle said. It was a place I'd never heard of. He hadn't told me where we were going.

Uncle got out his machete and hacked down a sapling at the side of the road. He trimmed it into a walking stick.

We started the descent to Nebaj, Uncle striding along, swinging the stick. The town had looked close, but the road down was long and winding. We got to a scattering of houses, and the dirt road fixed itself up fancy, just as a person would going to town. It became a street of smooth paving stones, lined with low houses painted in yellows and reds and blues.

The sun was low in the west, and the day was getting cool. We stood in the dark shadow of the houses. I took my shawl off my head and wrapped it around me. Uncle held out his walking stick, and I took hold of one end of it. I had to.

He was starting in on being blind.

I didn't mind so much when he got to a town and turned lame, or deaf and dumb. When he turned blind, that was the worst. He wouldn't tell me which way to go. But if I went the wrong way, he would get mad and poke at me with the stick.

"To the church," he said.

I guessed which way it was and walked ahead of him. Uncle followed, holding the other end of his walking stick, his chin raised high and a dead look in his eyes.

One day, we were in a town where I saw a girl helping her father, who was really blind, but you could hardly tell it. They walked side by side talking and sounding so happy, the father just lightly holding her arm. I listened, but I couldn't understand what they were saying, because they were speaking Mam, a language I don't know. Mostly I spoke Spanish like the ladinos do, but my first language was Mayan—Kaqchikel. If people didn't speak Spanish or Kaqchikel, I could understand only a little of what they said.

That day in the Mam-speaking town, the blind father and the girl turned off on a side street. I didn't see where they went, but I imagined them going to a white adobe house with a sky-blue door and red geraniums on the windowsills. I wondered if the girl's father worked. When they got home, did the girl's mother open the door and hug them? I made up a whole story about them in my head, and I told Uncle the way the blind man and the girl walked looked a lot easier and nicer than hauling a stick around.

That made him mad.

"Fool!" Uncle said. "Stupid sheep! What does a blind man know about being blind? Blind, and he isn't even getting the value out of it!"

2

The Plaza

The narrow street we were on led to the plaza at the center of town, with the white church looming over it. Above the church, I could see way up to the green mountains and the road where we'd come down. Curls of white fog on the mountainsides were spinning themselves into a blanket and drifting toward town.

The plaza was crowded with people, almost everybody Mayan. The men wore ladino clothes—jeans, factory-made shirts, and light jackets. The women and girls had stayed with the old ways. They wore handwoven clothes— huipiles all in red, but embroidered with other colors, and ankle-length red cortes wrapped around them and fastened with wide embroidered belts.

My own blouse and skirt had been woven in some different town, I didn't know which. Uncle had bought them secondhand.

When I was little, I'd had clothes that were mine first-hand, made especially for me. I'd watched my mother weave them. But those clothes I'd long ago outgrown, and Uncle had sold them.

He was looking around at the people in the plaza now, but pretending not to. All the children stayed close to their parents, holding their mothers' belts or their fathers' hands and the hands of little brothers and sisters, too. So nobody would get lost. In a family, everybody is connected.

I wondered if Uncle and I were connected like that. Held together with something besides his walking stick. Maybe we were. Maybe we just didn't know it.

The babies were riding against their mothers' backs, fastened in their mothers' shawls. They had on red bracelets and red wool caps to protect them from the cold night and from the evil eye.

Sometimes a person will envy a woman for having a beautiful baby and make the baby sick just by looking at it. To prevent that, the littlest babies were completely hidden, just tiny round shapes inside the soft wool of their mothers' shawls.

Was I carried like that once, so close to my mother?

Uncle cleared his throat and twisted the stick in his hand, signaling me to hurry up and cross the plaza. We got to the center of it, where there were lots of food stands with snacks. I walked as fast as I could down the aisle between the stands. Parents pulled their children near to let us pass.

Orange juice sellers were squeezing fresh juice into glasses, and washing used glasses in big buckets of water on the ground. Other vendors cooked little steaks and ears of corn over charcoal fires, and simmered plantains with sugar and cinnamon bark in big pots. Somewhere I could smell fresh potato sticks cooking in hot oil.

Uncle poked me to keep me walking.

We passed a table with little brown paper bags of potato sticks set out, a plastic squeeze bottle of green hot sauce in the middle of them. Then came an open space, and after that, the church, with concrete steps leading up to it and huge wide-open wooden doors.

"Four steps," I told Uncle, as if he couldn't see them for himself.

He climbed them and sat down as if he wasn't sure where the ground was, took off his hat and the carrying strap, and opened up the black suitcase. He got out the gray plastic begging bowl and set it down between us.

When we were on the road, Uncle was a man you would hardly notice, with his simple white shirt and black pants and his eyes cast down. But once he sat in front of a church or at the edge of a market to beg, he changed.

It was as if he reached into the air for a thick coat of

goodness and pulled it around himself and made himself bigger. You couldn't walk by him without noticing his humility. You would think he was a man who would never quarrel with anybody, and even if someone insulted him, he was so humble the insult would wash right off him. You would think he was a sober man, and if you gave him money he would never use it to get drunk, the way a lot of beggars do. You would think he would never steal from anyone, and if somebody dropped something valuable, he would return it to that person except for the terrible tragedy that he couldn't, he was blind.

Uncle was good at being deaf and dumb and lame, but he was an artist at being blind. Nobody who was blind ever looked as blind as he did, and nobody good ever looked so good. I'm not saying he did many bad things— he didn't, really. He didn't drink much, and he didn't get in fights, and even if we often didn't eat anything but bread or tortillas and salt for days at a time, still, he took care of me. It's just that when he pulled on his invisible coat of goodness, he looked so much bigger and so much better than he really was.

Families were coming toward the church in the twilight, bigger kids lifting the little ones whose legs were too short to climb the steps. Uncle raised his eyes to the grownups' faces, just as if he couldn't see them and only guessed where they might be.

I looked up too—serious and unsmiling—just the way he'd taught me. It was my job.

For a long time Uncle had tried to get me to help more when he begged—to say "Please, something for a blind man" or "Help my father, he can't see." But I couldn't say those things. When I tried, only strange sounds came out. Uncle scolded me, he said those sounds drove people away. But I couldn't stop. So finally he said I didn't need to try to do that job anymore.

When I was little, I did better. Then I lived with my family and my mother gave me my tasks. The first job she gave me was to be honest and not to say bad words. Then, to hold thread for her when she was weaving. To carry small logs to the cooking fire. To sweep the floor. To throw corn on the ground outside to feed the chickens. To chase them if they got into the garden. To open the door for my father when he came home at night and give him a happy greeting.

Jobs are very important in families. Everybody has to do the jobs right so a family can survive. At every mealtime, before my family ate, we each thanked one another for helping to make that meal.

Later, when I got used to being with Uncle, I wanted to help him with jobs, too. But I couldn't do any of the ones I knew. There was no door to open. I couldn't sweep because there wasn't a floor. There wasn't a chicken to chase or a flower or a carrot to protect. Sometimes at meals I tried to thank Uncle for his work, but he acted as if he didn't hear me or he didn't know the words. He never thanked me back.

In the end, my job was helping Uncle when he begged. He wished I'd do better at it. But he wasn't my father, so I couldn't say he was, and he wasn't blind, so I couldn't say he was. Because the first job my mother taught me was to be honest, and she would want to know, if I ever got back to her, that I'd done at least one job right.

3

The Man with the Beautiful Hat

Men entering the church took off their hats, while women covered their heads with their shawls. Women and children glanced at us and looked away. The men studied Uncle and me, trying to see if Uncle was really blind. A lot dropped money into our bowl—ten centavos or a choca—twenty-five centavos. Sometimes even a Guatemala quetzal bill.

If a coin fell, and Uncle could hear it land, he said, "May God reward you." But if someone dropped a paper bill, a quetzal, into the bowl, he didn't say anything, because he couldn't hear it and was pretending not to see it.

Then it was my job to say thank you. I said it the way Uncle taught me, in a low, sad voice.

The last glow of twilight was gone. The streetlights had come on.

From inside the church, I could hear a voice talking in a language I didn't understand. People entering late hurried past us.

It was a night like almost all the nights with Uncle, the nights that never changed.

A tickling breeze carried the sweetness and the saltiness of the fried potato sticks. My mouth was so dry I could hardly swallow, but still I longed for the potato sticks. Except for the bit of bread at the spring, I hadn't eaten since breakfast.

I hated my stomach. I wished there were no such thing as food or bodies that wanted it.

A Christian girl once told me about the Christian heaven. You don't ever get hungry there, if what she said is true.

She said when I died and left Earth, I would leave my body behind, but later I'd get back together with it, and in the meantime, God would have fixed it up. He'd say, "I've made this house of flesh for you; come in."

And it would be a perfect body that didn't need food. All cozy in that new body, I'd sit high above the Earth on a gold cushion on a cloud.

I would have a harp, the Christian girl said. I don't know how to play a harp, but the girl told me that, in heaven, you learn after you get there and at first it's okay if you just hold it.

Sitting on the top step of that church, I imagined being in my perfect body up on the highest clouds, so high a person on Earth would look no bigger than a grain of dust. I imagined gazing down on all those tiny people with my perfect eyes, and forgiving every single one for not caring about me.

Next to me, Uncle sat as motionless as if he'd been carved in stone. There was no way to know what he was thinking about. He didn't talk. He didn't even scratch if he itched.

A child who begs can move a little bit, but if a man moves when he begs, it spoils the impression. That's what Uncle always said.

The air got colder and had the stillness that comes before rain. Out of the corner of my eye I could see the cook who was making the potato sticks, hear the crackling every time she dumped a fresh handful into the hot oil. The smell of them rose into my nostrils and formed a cloud of hunger in my brain.

Tears dripped down my cheeks. I squeezed my eyes tight shut to stop them, but they still kept leaking out.

Fingers brushed my chin, then moved away.

I opened my eyes, and there was a man standing over me, a ladino with light skin and brown hair. He had on a soft wool jacket from a Kaqchikel town and a beautiful hat—not like the brittle old straw hat Uncle wore, but a velvety one that shone soft as the wing of a mountain dove.

"Why are you crying?" he said.

I didn't answer him. I didn't have the words to say why, and the strange creature that knots up and rises in my throat was ready to stop me if I tried.

The look in his eyes was soft and golden, as if he knew the reason I cried, and was sorry.

"What's your name?" he said.

I couldn't say "Rosa," at least not without stammering. "Tzunún," I told him, and the word came out fine. But I said it low so Uncle wouldn't hear it. Uncle used to get mad if I said I was Tzunún.

The ladino smiled. "How good to be named for the most beautiful creature God has made, the one that does no harm to anybody!" He reached into the pocket of his trousers.

He put money in my hand—a hundred-quetzal bill, brand-new. Not dirty like most paper money. It had never been bent or twisted or crumpled even once.

"For you," he said, "not for the begging bowl."

I could feel Uncle beside me watching, listening. He stayed blank and calm and still. Just once, his eyelids twitched.

"*Matiox*," I said to the ladino: "thank you" in Kaqchikel. Because of his jacket, I thought he might speak Kaqchikel.

He smiled and crinkly lines appeared at the corners of his eyes.

"*Kirik a*," he answered me. That was Kaqchikel, too. It

means "I'll see you again." "And if I don't have that good fortune," he added in Spanish, "I wish you well."

He took off his beautiful hat and hurried into the church.

I rubbed the one-hundred-quetzal bill with my fingertips, just to feel its cleanness. The white and the brown of it shone under the streetlights.

I rolled the bill so it wouldn't be creased and put it in the little cloth money bag I wear on a cord around my neck. It would be safe there. No one would ever guess I had it. It would be hidden under my huipil.

A song of triumph and joy burst from the church. Outside, the first raindrops fell from the cloudy sky. People who were still eating around the food stalls sheltered under their roofs of draped black plastic.

Uncle scooped the coins and small bills out of the gray bowl and put them in his pocket. He stuffed the bowl into the suitcase and took out the big sheets of blue plastic we wore as raincoats.

We draped ourselves in the plastic sheets.

Uncle held out a hand from under his.

"Give me the hundred."

"Un-Un-Uncle—the man said it was for me."

I turned my face toward Uncle. Raindrops struck my cheeks.

He glared down at me.

"When something is yours, I'll tell you."

"But the m-m-man said it was for me."

Uncle shook his head. "He's a sheep. He knows nothing. What he said means nothing."

I hunched my shoulders. I wanted to curl up into a ball and disappear. But I didn't give up.

"Un-Un-Un-cle! He gave it to me! It's mine."

"Forget what he said!" Uncle shouted.

He pulled his plastic sheet tighter, picked up his stick and the suitcase.

"You want to be on your own? You think you can take care of yourself? Then go!"

He turned his back.

I pulled out my little cloth bag, opened it, and got out the hundred. Uncle started walking, testing the wet ground with his stick, never looking back.

I ran after him through the spattering rain.

"U-Uncle! Uncle! T-t-take it!"

He stopped. He put the bill in his old black snake-skin wallet.

"Gracias." He smiled. In the light from the streetlamps his teeth gleamed yellow between dark spaces where he'd lost some. He handed me one end of his walking stick.

"Belly empty?" he said.

I didn't answer.

We sheltered under a food stall roofed with a green sheet of plastic.

He ordered for both of us—a blood-red sweet tea made from boiled flower petals; corn on the cob with mayonnaise and ketchup over it; steak and tortilla sandwiches;

and, just for me, one whole bag of potato sticks with green hot sauce.

I ate my food with my cold wet fingers, listening to the rain, thinking of the man with the beautiful hat, his touch that had been so soft, his voice that had been so kind. The memory of him was like a flower dying.

Times before I had met people who were beautiful, and never seen them again. The man with the beautiful hat would be another.

Uncle wiped his lips with the back of his hand and pointed across the street. I led him through the rain to a bakery. Uncle shifted his plastic sheet so the water would run off. Behind the counter, there were cabinets with glass doors where all the different kinds of bread were kept.

Rain was thundering down on the tin roof of the bakery. Uncle shouted to be heard.

"What do you want, Rosa, a swan? Do they have the swans?"

"Yes, Uncle."

He knew those were my favorites, the golden-brown rolls shaped to look like swans, with round heads and long graceful necks.

"Two," Uncle said.

"For here or to go?" the woman said.

"For here," Uncle said.

The woman gave us each a roll and Uncle paid her.

"Gracias, Uncle," I said. I ate mine with the tiniest

possible bites, starting at the back, because it always made me sad to see the swan without a head.

First thing, Uncle tore the head off his and chomped it in one bite.

That's the way he liked to do it, every time.

4

Morning in Nebaj

Under a portico on the south side of the church, Uncle and I huddled in our blankets. I watched the rain slide off high dark branches of cypress trees and dance on the shining black stones of the street.

When I finally slept, I dreamed about the man with the beautiful hat. He and Uncle were in the bakery talking, and I was listening.

"You're a beggar," the man with the beautiful hat told Uncle, "but the girl's not."

I didn't understand why he said that. A beggar is someone who begs, I wanted to tell him, but in the dream I couldn't talk.

"She's just like me," Uncle said. "I keep her because she owes me a great treasure. Eight years now I'm waiting!"

For years I'd known that he expected me to find him a

treasure. I would have done it, too, if I'd known where to look.

The man with the beautiful hat frowned. "She owes you nothing!"

I hoped Uncle didn't believe him. If Uncle believed I didn't owe him any treasure, he might leave me.

Uncle bragged, "Rosa's going to lead me to riches like you've never seen!"

"You think that will make you happy? It won't," the ladino said.

That surprised me. I always thought that if only I could find the treasure, Uncle would be happy and I'd be happy, too.

I wanted to ask the stranger why the treasure wouldn't make Uncle happy. I tried to speak so hard the trying woke me. Then the sun walked around yellow inside my head, licking my dream till it dissolved.

Uncle was packing away his blankets, whistling snatches of a song about a man who lived like a stone in a road, learning to be hard, to roll on and on. After a little bit, the line "Roll on and on" was the only one he kept whistling.

I didn't much like it, but I guess he did.

I helped him close up the suitcase, and we started downtown, me leading with the stick. A lot of people had seen Uncle being blind the night before, so he had to stay that way.

We smelled soap and saw a big public pila—the place

where women who don't have running water at home gather to wash their families' clothes.

The pila was made out of concrete, with a deep reservoir of water like a swimming pool in the center and individual concrete sinks around it. Women were scrubbing clothes with bright orange balls of laundry soap.

They gave us permission to use an empty sink to wash our hands and faces. I got our orange soap out of the suitcase, and a woman poured water into the sink for us. After we'd washed, she gave us directions to the market on the other side of town.

At the market everything you could think of was for sale, spread out on long tables or on the ground—handmade wooden chairs, heaps of hoes and hammers and every kind of tool, plastic sandals, silverware, dishes, dark glasses, music tapes, watches, toothpaste; beautiful flowers in buckets of water; fruits and vegetables, hunks of red meat dangling from steel hooks, and dried plants to cure all kinds of illnesses.

A market is the cheapest place to eat. What Uncle wanted was breakfast.

He twisted the stick a little when we passed the eating place he preferred, one with a table and a bench, where two men and a woman were already sitting. On the other side of the table a woman was waiting on everyone as she cooked over a charcoal grill on the ground.

Uncle gave me his stick and slid onto the bench,

crowding everybody and greeting them with a big "Buenos días." He pretended not to see some plants growing in powdered milk tins, which were for sale at his end of the table, and almost knocked them over.

The cook moved the plants a little bit and said, "There, there, señor, no problem," and the young man next to Uncle guided his hand so he could feel where the plants were and wouldn't hit them again. Uncle said gracias.

I pushed our suitcase under the table where nobody could steal it. There wasn't any room for me on the bench, so I stood at the end of the table. Pointy leaves on the plants tickled my arms. A woman with two shopping baskets and a man with a wheelbarrow full of raw steaks and vegetables squeezed through the space behind me.

The cook cleared dirty dishes off the table and stuck them into a bucket of soapy water on the ground.

I looked at the pots on the grill and told Uncle what she was serving. He ordered me tortillas with hot sauce and coffee with a lot of sugar in it. He ordered the same for himself, plus a bowl of black bean soup.

The woman and the two men next to Uncle looked at him and commented in Ixil, I don't know what, but I thought they were saying something that was no compliment to Uncle.

Uncle ate most of the soup and held the bowl out for me. The cook scooped some extra beans into the bowl and gave me a clean spoon.

"Your girl is very thin," the cook said to Uncle, "but I suppose you don't see that."

"Always been a skinny one," Uncle replied cheerfully. "Like a bird."

He munched a tortilla, then stuck his head forward and spoke loud.

"I have a question. Is there anyone who can answer a question?" He could have been announcing some important contest, speaking to a big crowd. It seemed as if he didn't know there were only three people sitting by him.

They didn't answer. Maybe they thought he was some kind of preacher, talking loud like that. Maybe he'd ask if they believed in Jesus, if they believed, mistakenly, that they were without sin. Or maybe he'd ask if anyone could lend him money, because of a personal emergency.

Uncle lowered his voice a little and sounded less important. "I want somebody to recommend a Day-Keeper, that's all."

I had never met any Day-Keepers, but I'd heard of them. Some have magical powers, and what you say bad about them may rebound against you. All of them keep track of the old Mayan calendar—the one the Christians tried to abolish—and that's important, some people say, because the old calendar holds the secrets of our lives.

Because of the old calendar, the Day-Keepers know exactly when to take people to shrines in the mountains to pray and leave offerings for the earth spirits. To leave

sugar, or rum, or maybe a clean-plucked chicken as an offering.

The spirit doesn't actually come out of his hill to eat
chicken. The spirit gets fed by magic. But it knows a person has gone to the trouble to make the sacrifice, to show
respect, and that matters to the spirit.

Even though he'd lowered his voice, the people on the
bench didn't answer Uncle right away. Maybe it was because they didn't trust him. Or maybe it was because of
the war—the big war here in Guatemala before I was
born. Back then a lot of people who said the wrong thing
in front of the wrong stranger died. In many places people still don't like to talk much to strangers.

"Nobody will tell me?" Uncle said, in a weak, com-
plaining voice.

The people on the bench looked at one another. I could
see they felt a little ashamed of not helping a blind guy.

The young man sitting next to Uncle said, "Jerónimo
Sic could do a ceremony for you."

At the other end of the bench, an older, skinny man
grimaced. He turned around to see who might overhear
him and kept silent, but I could tell from his face that he
didn't respect Jerónimo Sic.

"Jerónimo's all right," the younger man insisted.

The skinny man looked glum, as if he already knew
that one more time he was going to say what he thought
because he couldn't stop himself.

"Jerónimo's a chicken-eater."

"Not so, brother!" the younger man argued. "The real chicken-eater is Martín Chai."

The woman between them swung her head, red tassels bobbing on the ribbon wound into her hair.

"My cousin Martín knows a lot!" she said.

"Even so," the younger man said, "he never had a gift or a dream, and despite all he knows, he's still a chicken-eater."

That's about the worst name you can call anyone who deals in magic. A chicken-eater will take a client to a shrine to offer a chicken—but later sneak back, steal the chicken, and roast it for dinner at his own house, not caring one bit about the spirits in the hill.

The people on the bench had all forgotten about Uncle and me being strangers. They would have argued a good long time if the cook hadn't interrupted.

"Forget Jerónimo and Martín," she told Uncle, wiping her hands on her apron. "Señor, you should go to Celestina Tuc. I'm a Christian and I still go see her. She's a very good woman and God talks to her."

"It's true Celestina's good," the woman said. "I never heard anybody say a bad word about her. Some people say she changes the future."

"She may," the glum man said, "but she's not one who would ever say so. Not like most who boast of magical deeds they've never done."

"All I want is to know the plain and simple future,"

Uncle said. "If she can tell me that, I'll be happy." He paid the cook for breakfast, fingering each coin as if that were the only way he knew its value, and asked the way to Celestina Tuc's house.

We followed a narrow lane between hibiscus hedges, the bright red petals of their flowers folded closed like butterfly wings. Uncle hurried, carrying his stick over his shoulder, not even pretending to be blind. In the middle of the lane, little kids crouched by puddles, floating tiny boats made of corn husks. Chickens wandered out of dirt yards behind the hedges, and Uncle weighed them with his eyes.

In his own way, he was a chicken-eater himself, but he took live ones. If we were leaving a town and one crossed the road when nobody was looking, he'd wring its neck and stick it in his rope bag.

I used to believe him when he said that the chickens he took were wild ones—the only wild chickens in Guate-mala.

Uncle passed by the chickens in this lane, though. He knew he couldn't show up at a Day-Keeper's house with a neighbor's dead chicken still warm in his bag.

We got to a dark blue wooden gate. Beyond the gate we could see big flowerpots with pink begonias in them. Trellises supporting the vines of golden-orange flowers people call Necklaces of the Queen made a roof over the entry path.

Uncle pulled on the bell rope next to the gate, and a bell somewhere deep in the yard jingled.

Uncle put on his honest look and peered toward the house to see who was coming.

I didn't. Fortune-tellers and black-magic people and all kinds of priests scared me. I knew about Day-Keepers, but I didn't want to meet one.

"When she comes, I'll stay outside. I'll wait for you," I told Uncle.

I thought that would be all right with him. But no— for once, he wanted me along.

5

The Club and the Princess

Lots of times, when Uncle wasn't begging, he didn't want me around. He'd give me a bunch of small change so I could eat, and he'd go away for a day or two, drinking and trying to win at cards, looking for girlfriends, or working on his luck and getting his fortune told.

He didn't stick with drinking, because he didn't have the money. He didn't stick with cards, because after a while he lost. He didn't stick with a girlfriend, because he lost with girlfriends, too. Eventually they wanted to know what he worked at, and they didn't like it when they found out.

The only thing he really stuck with was working on his luck. That was the most important thing, the one thing he never gave up. I was the reason.

Right after he found me, I was so sad and crying all the

time, he took me to a room with a curtain pulled so I would sleep.

He asked me how old I was, and I told him I was four. He was surprised. He said, "You're little for your age."

He asked me my name.

"Tzunún Chumil." Hummingbird Star. In case he didn't know that "Tzunún" meant "hummingbird," I told him in Spanish: "Colibrí."

He smiled. He said "Tzunún" was too hard for him to say, and so was "Colibrí." He was going to call me Rosa.

He said he had many names, so the best name I could call him would be "Uncle."

"Say it," he coaxed. "Say 'Uncle.' "

I looked at the window. The curtain must have been white once, but it was gray from age and soot. Around it an edge of sunlight struggled in.

I remember that day very well, because that's when the trouble started with my voice. I wanted to repeat what he said, but I couldn't.

"Say it. Say 'Uncle.' "

I had an uncle, but he was not the one.

"Say it. Say 'Uncle,' and you can have a cookie."

He smiled, but just with his teeth.

He showed me the cookie. "See, it's a nice big one."

"I want my mother."

"Your mother lost you," he said. "Your mother didn't want you. Say 'Uncle.' "

I couldn't say it.

"I can't wait all day for you," he said.

He put the cookie on top of a tall clothes cupboard. Then he went out. I don't know how long it was before he came back, except that it was almost night and there was no sunlight shining in under the curtain.

He opened the door and switched on a light. He smiled at me and got down the cookie. My mouth was dry. I swallowed and swallowed and swallowed again.

There was something in my mouth that was not part of me, but no matter how I tried to touch it with my tongue, I couldn't find it. And no matter how many times I swallowed, it stayed there.

"Water, too," he said. "You can have some water. Just say 'Uncle.' "

"U-U-Uncle," I said.

From that time I could always say "Uncle." But I never knew when it would happen, when the something that was not me would be in my mouth, choking me.

The next day he brought me a doll, and he kept the curtain open longer.

A few days later he said he wanted me to be happy, so he took me to a fair.

I never saw a fair before. There was fluffy pink candy like wool on a stick. There were giant men on stilts with purple hair and peaked hats and painted smiles red as blood.

There were huge machines with steel arms and steel hands that went around people and snatched them off the ground. High up in the air, round and round they went, laughing and screaming and hanging on tight to the iron hands. I had Uncle's hand. I held it very tight.

We went through a curtain into a little tent. It was full of diamond-shaped mirrors in gold frames, and black candles burning. A lady was going to tell us something important.

Uncle said a word to her that I didn't know—*adoption*. The lady frowned. "I don't arrange that. I don't know about that. Who sent you here?"

He said somebody had told him.

She said, "And you want to get your thirty pieces of silver, no doubt?"

"It's a favor to the child," Uncle said.

The lady asked me my name.

"Tzunún Chumil. 'Tzunún' means 'Colibrí.' "

"My, you know a lot!" the lady said, and she smiled at me, but not for long.

"Do you know where you live, Tzunún?"

"Yes," I said.

She smiled at me. "And where do you live, Tzunún?"

"I live in San," I said.

"That's your town?"

"Yes."

"But San can't be the whole name," the lady said. "San Diego? San Francisco? San what?"

I knew there was more to it than just "San," but I couldn't remember what.

"Well, that's too bad," the lady said. "I'm sorry you can't remember the rest."

She hissed at Uncle. "Simpleton! The foreigners want babies. She's too old, far too old."

I didn't know who the lady was talking about or what "simpleton" meant.

Uncle shrugged. "So what should I do?"

"That's your problem, not mine," the lady said. "You might see what the cards say. It's only two quetzales."

Uncle said all right.

She had cards with pictures on them that she laid out on a table. Some were pretty. Some were not. One had a black-haired princess on it with her hands full of sparkling yellow jewels, so many they were falling out in all directions. Another card showed a huge knobby club, all bulging with thorns.

The lady looked at all the cards, dealing them out this way and that. The princess card always ended up on top of the card with the club.

"This I've never seen," she said to Uncle. "Your fortune and hers are braided. What happens in one life depends on what happens in the other."

With a ringed finger, she pointed to the club and its thorns. "This is the luck of a poor man," she said. "But on top of it is this . . ." She held up the card with the black-haired princess and the jewels.

"Here is the child," she said, "of course, a little older than she is now. The cards say she's going to make you rich. But you must be good to her."

After we left that lady, Uncle was very good to me for a long time. He fed me. When my feet grew, he bought me new plastic sandals. When the clothes my mother had made for me were all too small, and I cried because I couldn't wear them anymore, he bought me new ones.

When he went out to beg, I would sit with him. People thought he was a blind widower, who took good care of his daughter. Sometimes they told him so. Because of me they gave him coins. But I never made him rich.

When he won at cards or got extra money, he would spend it to improve his luck. He would talk to Mayan priests and to black-magic men. He would pay for sacrifices of rum and black candles made with pig fat to the evil saint, San Simón Judas, who sold Jesus Christ for thirty pieces of silver. He would make pure sacrifices of cleaned chickens and green candles of bee's wax to the Ahau, the Lord God of the Maya.

Priests and black-magic men would tell him yes, he was going to be rich, he only had to wait a little longer.

He'd ask how long, and they would say, "The Ahau is never in a hurry." Or, "God's time is not man's."

One night we were between towns, camped in a pasture under the stars. I was about ten by then. Uncle was drinking rum and talking a lot. He told me about all the sacrifices he had made to help get the riches I was supposed to bring him. He asked me if I saw gold or silver in my dreams, if any special place attracted me, because we could visit it. I said no.

Uncle groaned and put his head in his hands. He looked up at the stars and asked the Ahau and the good and bad saints why he was keeping me. They didn't answer.

But he didn't give me up. Just like the fight in his blood, the treasure had him stuck. He didn't completely believe in it, but he couldn't get rid of his hope. Probably that's why he kept me.

But maybe also, he couldn't stand to be alone.

6

The Day-Keeper

The woman at the gate was slender, with a beautiful proud face. She reminded me of mountains—the way they are immovable, the way they are complete in themselves and yet seem to watch.

Uncle bowed a little. "Good morning," he said. "Would you be Señora Celestina Tuc?"

"I am," she said. Her eyes took in Uncle, his stick, the battered suitcase, and me. "You're carrying a lot. You've come a long way."

"True," Uncle said.

"And why?"

"People told me the Day-Keepers of Nebaj are the wisest," Uncle said.

"Gracias," Señora Tuc said.

"I want to know about my future," Uncle said.

"Everybody wants to know the future," Señora Tuc said, smiling. "At least, they think they do. But there's a price."

Uncle hunched his shoulders. "What do you charge? I have little."

"I'm not talking about money," Señora Tuc said. "All knowledge has another kind of price. One way or another, we have to pay the universe for it. As far as *my* price—I'll help you with pleasure—just give what you wish."

"Gracias, señora," Uncle said. He smiled, glad she didn't want much. I figured he wasn't worried at all about having to pay the universe. We moved around so much, I didn't see how the universe was ever going to catch up with him and show a bill.

"You don't believe me about the universe," Señora Tuc said. "But, señor, you'll see—one day the universe will charge you."

She unlatched the gate. We followed her under the golden-orange flowers to the house and into a large bare room. Uncle set his stick and suitcase down by the door.

The floor of the room was made of small colored tiles that formed a mosaic of green corn plants and blue sky. In the sky, all in a circle, were the sun, the moon, the planets, and the stars. Near one white wall were two chairs and a small table. There was a thick book on the table, and a cloth bag embroidered in red and yellow.

Señora Tuc gestured to a long bench against the opposite wall. We sat down on it, under a window. Uncle took off his old straw hat and held it on his lap, bending the brim up and down in his hands.

Señora Tuc asked him if he knew anything about the old ways.

"Not so much," he said.

She took reading glasses from her huipil and put them on. She carried the thick book over to Uncle so he could see it close up. It had pages and pages of writing in it, all in neat black columns.

"This is a book of one of the old calendars," she said, "—the one with twenty months of thirteen days. It's been kept for thousands of years."

"I heard of it," Uncle said, "but I don't know how it works."

"Every month has its own special character that it gives to the people born in it. Each day from one to thirteen has its own effect, too."

She turned many pages, ran her finger along rows of numbers. "The book shows the correlation between the Christian calendar dates and the ancient ones."

Uncle stared at the book, his lips moving as he tried to read a page.

"It won't do you any good to read it," Señora Tuc said. "You're reading just the correlations, not the meaning.

"The important thing is the days," she said. "They have

a power. They're part of the seed a new life grows from. They shape the life. A person will always have the character of the days of his conception and his birth."

Uncle made a juicy sucking sound, running his tongue down his front teeth. "I hear the days give luck to some people. Maybe I am one."

"I hope so for your sake," the Day-Keeper said.

Uncle smiled. He looked away from Señora Tuc, down at the mosaic of corn plants and stars. Light from the window glanced off the bald spot on the top of his head.

Señora Tuc's face tensed. "I've seen you before!" she said.

"It can't be," Uncle said.

"Yes! In the war years," Señora Tuc insisted. "You were much younger, but already losing your hair."

Uncle gripped the patched knees of his trousers. "No, señora. I've never been here."

"Not here, but close by. I saw you! You were a soldier on an army truck with other soldiers. There was blood on your clothes. You were coming from La Hortensia plantation. I noticed you because you were so young, but already a little bald on the top of your head."

"I never heard of La Hortensia," Uncle said.

Señora Tuc considered, shrugged. "It was a long time ago. I saw the young man who looked like you only for an instant. Maybe it wasn't you."

"It wasn't, señora, believe me," Uncle said.

"I'm glad to hear it." She sat down again at the table. "So now, today, what do you want?"

"I came to find out if one certain thing will happen. If it will happen, when it will happen."

"Before I can tell you anything, I need to know your name."

Uncle uncrossed his legs and stuck his feet out, scraping his shoes against the tiles on the floor. "Lucas Dardón," he said.

When he had to use a name, that was one of the ones he used.

"If you give me false information, I will give you false information!" Señora Tuc snapped.

I didn't know how she had guessed he was telling a lie.

She sat with the left side of her face in shadow, the right side catching the light from the window. Lines jagged as lightning flashes zigzagged across the bright side of her face. The shadowed side seemed only to wait and watch and know.

Uncle put on his thick look of being good, leaving not one patch or hole to see through.

"In truth, my name is Baltasar Om."

I never heard him give that name before. Maybe it was the real one.

The Day-Keeper nodded. Her eyes didn't focus on his clean white shirt, his heavy black shoes, or his invisible coat of waxy goodness. Her eyes roved about his edges—

the way a person looks around a spider to see the full size of its web. As if beyond Uncle's coat of goodness she was looking for something else.

"And what is the girl's name?"

"Rosa Garcia. She's my niece. I take care of her."

"She's not your niece," Señora Tuc said. "I don't know what her name is, but that's not it!"

"That's the name she goes by," Uncle said. "She's like a niece to me. I take care of her."

Señora Tuc looked at me. The strange thing in my throat rose up, choking me. I wondered if it was a demon, if there was a way the Day-Keeper could get rid of it. Or if there was no way to ever get rid of it.

With my eyes I begged her not to ask me anything, not to make Uncle angry.

"Don't worry, m'hija," she said. "My daughter," she was saying. Strangers being kind call children "my daughter" or "my son," as if they are including them in their family, as if all human beings are one family. But almost nobody spoke like that to me.

She looked around me, the same way she had looked at Uncle, as if her eyes were reading the air. My hands fluttered upward, clutched my throat.

"Rosa doesn't talk much," Uncle said. "It's hard for her. It's a problem in her gullet."

The Day-Keeper smiled at me. "It will be better, child, don't worry. —And, Baltasar, your birth date."

He told her.

I never heard his birth date before. Maybe the one he said was the real one. We never celebrated his birthday, so I didn't know. It would have been nice if between the two of us, one of us at least had a birthday.

Señora Tuc beckoned Uncle to the table and told him to take a chair. She ran her finger over a page in the book.

"You see here, Señor Om, your birth date is 10 Imox. I'm sorry to say it's not a good day. It's the day of someone who is obsessed, yet who isn't sure about his thoughts, who changes his mind all the time. The birth date of someone who doesn't pay his debts."

I thought Uncle would say he wasn't like that, but he didn't. He only shifted his weight in the chair and pulled his feet in.

"We're not to blame for the faults we're born with," the Day-Keeper said, "but we need to struggle against them. Maybe you've done that?"

She looked at him inquiringly, but Uncle said nothing.

Señora Tuc closed her book. "From the day influences, I see your job is being a waiter."

Uncle slapped his hands against his knees in disgust, unsettling his hat so it dropped to the floor. "Not at all! Never. I don't slave for anyone!"

"You may not be a waiter in a restaurant," the Day-Keeper said, "but you wait at the table of life. You wait for the crumbs to fall. Maybe a whole rich cake will fall!" She smiled.

"But in any case, if you want to know what's coming, I

44

can consult my little seeds. They'll tell what will happen—the thing you want to know. Would you like a reading of the seeds?"

Uncle picked his hat up off the floor. "I would. What is it that I have to do?"

"It's not hard," the Day-Keeper said. "Just focus on your question, Baltasar Om."

7

The Seeds

Uncle's fleshy eyelids closed. A furrow formed between his eyebrows.

Señora Tuc picked up the embroidered bag from the table, kissed it, and held her hands over it. Her eyes seemed to focus far away, outside the window, deep in the sky.

She untied the bag and emptied it. Shiny and bright red, a heap of seeds a little smaller than corn kernels fell into her palm. There was something cheerful and friendly about them, as if they wanted to do their work.

Señora Tuc noticed me straining to see. "Come stand closer, m'hija, if you wish to."

Uncle opened his eyes. I got up and came to stand at his shoulder.

"Everything in nature is alive, the seeds, too," Señora

Tuc explained. "They'll indicate the days, the months, the years involved in your question. The ancestors will be present, too. They'll tell me more."

She laid the seeds in a heap on the table and asked Uncle to pick up as many as he could with one sweep of his right hand.

"Don't calculate," she said; "just gather some."

Uncle's eyes glittered the way they had when he looked at the chickens in the lane. He *was* calculating, figuring out how to gather every last seed. He grabbed so many he couldn't hold them all and some dribbled from his closed fist.

"Don't worry, those don't matter," Doña Celestina said. She set the spilled seeds to one side. She told Uncle to put those he still held in a mound in the middle of the table.

She arranged the little red seeds in groups of two, in five rows. In the last little pile, there was only one seed. She studied the arrangement and she put all the seeds together, including the ones she'd set aside. She had Uncle pick up as many seeds as he could a second time. Those, too, she arranged in rows—four rows of paired seeds. Again, one seed was left over, sitting by itself.

She considered the seeds one more time, then put them away in her bag, and kissed it reverently.

Uncle eyed the bag on the table, waiting for her to speak, his eyes big in the shadows of the room.

"Baltasar, your question is whether you will be rich or not. Am I not right?"

"True," Uncle said. "And will I?" His voice cracked hoarsely.

"You will indeed."

"Excelente!" Uncle said.

"But the seeds show you have many debts. You have a debt to Mundo."

"Five hundred," Uncle said.

That was the truth. I knew that. He had owed his friend Raimundo five hundred quetzales for years.

Señora Tuc shook her head. "It's not Raimundo, your friend, I'm talking about," she said. "Your debt is to Mundo, the world. The mountains, the animals, the plants, the air that feeds your lungs—all that is Mundo."

Uncle frowned. "Mundo isn't God," he said.

"There's only one God," Doña Celestina said, "but he has two thousand names."

"I didn't come to hear about religion," Uncle said.

"We were speaking of debts," Señora Tuc said. "You have a debt to this girl, too."

Uncle frowned at me. He rubbed his nose resentfully, and scraped his shoes across the floor. "A debt? Indeed, it's thanks to me she eats!"

"You must be grateful to her," Doña Celestina insisted. "You must treat her well. She is the one who will make you rich. She's going to find a treasure for you.

"However, you owe her. You owe her a little paper. That's what I see."

"How rich will I be?" Uncle asked. His eyes were glittering again, darting rapidly to see every detail of the room in case the treasure was somewhere around us.

"Rich enough for any man."

"This is sure?" Uncle said.

"The seeds and the ancestors speak clearly. You'll live rich to the end of your days."

Uncle forgot the lecture about debts and smiled; he couldn't help himself. "Priests and magic women and men have told me this before. But they never say when I will get the treasure. That's what I really want to know."

"Soon," the Day-Keeper said.

"Soon in God's time, or in man's time?"

"In man's time. Within a year in the old calendar."

"How many days is that?"

"Only two hundred sixty."

Uncle leaned toward her, licking his lips. "You're certain?"

"Yes," Señora Tuc said. "The little seeds know how to mark the days. They never lie."

"Did they tell anything more?" Uncle asked.

The Day-Keeper hesitated, folded her hands.

"There is one sign that's bad."

"And what is that?" Uncle asked.

"You saw it. At the end of laying out the seeds in rows, one seed was always left standing alone."

"And what does that mean?"

"Someone's going to be alone. It may not be you."

"¡Qué me importa!" Uncle laughed. "What do I care who's alone, as long as I'm rich?"

He stood up, a man without worries, and put on his hat.

"Gracias, señora," he said. He took his wallet out and handed her a bill.

She held it up to the light. It was a hundred, I could see, but the paper was flimsy, the colors faded and the figures blurred.

The Day-Keeper smiled at Uncle, raising her eyebrows.

"Gracias, Señor Om. You are too generous. May things go well for you."

But the tone of her voice cut like a knife. She meant the opposite of what she said, I was sure of that. That's what the magic people do sometimes. They say one thing, but inside their own minds they ask the ancestors and Mundo and the Ahau to understand in reverse.

Uncle didn't notice. He was still smiling, ready to go, picking up his suitcase and his stick. I didn't move. I could tell there was something more to settle between them.

"May you be paid as you give, but double," Doña Celestina said, her voice like a dagger.

Even Uncle had to notice, had to decide whether or not to be afraid.

He set down his suitcase and the stick. He ran his palm over his forehead.

"Pardon me, señora, I must have been confused. I didn't mean to give you that bill. Perhaps you don't like it because it's old. It's good, I assure you, but I have a new one that's better-looking." He took the faded, limp one from her hand.

"This is the bill I meant to give you, señora," he said, bowing his head, holding out a crisp new hundred.

He never had any money that looked that good. It had to be my hundred.

The Day-Keeper thanked him and set the new bill on her table, by the bag of seeds.

"Come on, Rosa," Uncle said.

He picked up his things again, and I got my shawl from the bench. Señora Tuc walked with us to the gate and wished us a good journey.

Uncle was disappearing around the first curve in the lane when she called out to him.

"Señor Om! One last thing: beware of water."

Uncle was jabbing his stick against the dirt, taking giant strides toward the future. He didn't turn around.

I was far behind him, hurrying after. *Did you hear what she said?* I was going to ask him. *Did you hear?*

I caught up with him.

I could have spoken. The coiled-up thing that so often uncoiled and swelled to fill my throat wasn't bothering me. It was coiled away into nothing.

I could have told him.

Beware of water, I could have said.

But I didn't.

8

Paper

Back on the street, Uncle went blind again. We passed a lot of stores, their walls all painted in pretty colors with images of what was for sale inside—so you'd know even if, like me, you couldn't read.

We got to a building decorated with just writing, no pictures. Uncle halted behind me, jerking the stick from my hand. He wanted to go in there.

"Two high steps," I said, just in case anyone was listening. He tapped with his stick on the sidewalk and then on the steps to see how high they were. I stood back so he could go in first.

Under the long glass counter inside were clocks and calculators and pens and all kinds of things of no use to us.

The ladino clerk behind the counter had pale hands

and soft fingers, two of them stroking his little mustache, maybe to help it grow better.

Uncle looked blindly around.

"Señor, señora," he said, "would you show the girl a little paper?"

There was a lot of it on shelves behind the clerk.

"What kind of paper?" asked the clerk. "Loose sheets? Letter paper?"

Uncle hadn't thought about kinds. "A small notebook," he said finally.

The clerk got five different ones and laid them on the counter in front of me. The prettiest had a hard shiny cover with a jungle painting on the front.

"That one with a toucan," I said. "I like it."

The clerk told Uncle the price.

"I'll take it," Uncle said.

"Do you perhaps need a writing instrument of some sort?" the clerk asked politely. But I thought he was laughing at us behind his mustache because he guessed we didn't own a pen or even a pencil.

Uncle nodded and told me to pick out a ball-point, so I did.

The clerk said, "¿Algo más? Anything more?"

Uncle said no. The clerk stuck the notebook and the pen into a plastic bag.

I put the bag in my shawl. I'd never had a pen before. Or paper, either. I didn't really know what I would do with them.

We went to the market next. Uncle pointed me to a little store attended by a wrinkled old lady with a patch over one eye.

At the counter he asked for cold Pepsis.

The old lady limped to a dusty white refrigerator in the corner, moving as if the ground were burning. Every time she lifted a foot, that seemed to give her some relief, but then right away the other foot had to touch down and take its turn to suffer.

She poured the Pepsis into two plastic bags and stuck straws in them, so we could carry them away and not have to pay the bottle deposit. I held the Pepsi bags while Uncle got out his money.

He set down the same flimsy hundred he had offered the Day-Keeper.

The old lady looked at it. "So much money for so little," she grumbled.

"I don't have change," Uncle said.

The old lady glowered at us and at the Pepsis, plump and brown in their bags. There was no way she could undo the sale and pour them back into the bottles to sell again.

She felt the bill with calloused fingers. She held it up to the light.

I was worried she would figure out that the bill was false. At the same time I almost wanted her to, because her feet hurt and she couldn't see well, and it wasn't fair that she was getting cheated. I didn't dare tell her, though, because if I had, Uncle would have said I was a liar and a troublemaker and then made me go without food.

"I'll take it," the old lady said. She dug down into a zippered pocket in her huipil and slowly counted out the change.

Probably someone else would take the bill from her as real. Probably she wouldn't lose by it.

When I was little and Uncle did things that weren't right, I used to try to talk to my mother in my mind and ask forgiveness, and I would imagine her forgiving me and holding me in her arms. But there were so many things that weren't right, I couldn't keep on going into all the details. In a corner of my mind I just told her "It wasn't my idea," as I led Uncle away fast, the Pepsi bags sloshing in my hand.

We detoured through lots of alleys so the old lady couldn't send anyone after us if she got suspicious. We turned in at a restaurant with five tables, a few flies, and no customers.

The waitress didn't like it that we were in her place drinking Pepsi we'd brought in from the street, but right away Uncle ordered a big meal of tortillas, rice, and chicken in a sauce of roasted pumpkin seeds, so she didn't complain.

Uncle didn't bother to play blind. He moved the salt dish and the chile sauce bottles off to the side of the table and said he was going to teach me writing.

He opened up my new notebook and drew some shapes

that looked mostly round like balls. He said they were vowels, and then he drew a bunch mostly shaped like crossed sticks and said they were consonants. He told me all the letters in a certain order that he said was the "alphabet," and he had me say them after him.

I asked him if he would write my name. He wrote: Rosa.

"My real name," I said. "Tzunún Chumil."

He looked surprised, but he didn't get angry when I said it, the way he had when I was little, and he wrote my real name down.

There was a Christian calendar on the wall, with a photo of volcanoes. Uncle got up to look at it, turning its pages and slowly counting out 260 days.

I sat staring at the notebook and the letters of my real name.

Right below where Uncle had written it, I copied it. Tzunún Chumil. Tzunún Chumil. Finally I got the letters just the way he'd done them. I was proud—but they looked strange and far away, as if they belonged to some other world where a girl named Tzunún Chumil was real.

That night in the churchyard I lay awake in my blankets thinking about so many things. I wondered about the man with the beautiful hat, and what my dream about him meant.

I wondered about other mysteries, too: how the Day-

Keeper knew I'd make Uncle rich, and how I ever could; and how a person could have a debt to the world.

Beyond the shelter of the church portico, raindrops dove at the ground, then stopped their suicidal falling, turning themselves to mist. I sensed Mundo, the Earth— one giant planet-animal, the mist his breath, his head the sky, his paws the mountains. I could feel his bigness, but also his lightness—the way he rested after rain as if he laid his burdens down.

9

I Visit the Day-Keeper

Uncle was still sleeping, his blankets twisted around his middle, one hand flung out across the suitcase. It was early yet, and in all the churchyard and the plaza there was nobody around.

I sat in my blankets looking at Uncle, waiting for him to wake up. I felt lonesome. When Uncle and I were in bigger places, sleeping under archways and bridges with other people, I was happier. There were more people to talk to then, and some of them were nice to me.

Uncle's eyes opened. "Rosa," he said, as if he was reminding himself that I existed. He searched in his pocket for his wallet, pulled it out, and handed me some coins.

"I couldn't sleep for thinking of that treasure. Go eat and let me rest." He covered his face with his blanket.

I straightened my clothes and combed my hair and

started off across the empty plaza, carrying my notebook and my pen in my shawl, thinking of eating at the market but not daring to, because of the old woman with the eye patch.

She might have told her friends, "Find me a blind man and a girl—the only girl wearing blue, she's the one."

I walked along, saying buenos días to the people I met, rubbing my cold arms under my shawl, hurrying just to keep myself warm. When I crossed the lane that led to the Day-Keeper's house I felt as if I'd been heading that way on purpose without knowing it.

I wanted to see her, I didn't know why. But I was afraid, too. I never visited anybody's house. I was hardly ever even *in* a house, the way Uncle and I lived.

I turned down the lane, walking along the edge of it, trying to avoid the wettest ground. I brushed against the hibiscus hedges, feeling the red flowers paint raindrops on my arm.

The worst the Day-Keeper could do would be to put some kind of spell on me, or talk to the ancestors about me in reverse language. But why would she? Even if she didn't like me, I wasn't worth that trouble.

I got to her gate and put my hand on the bell rope. First I was going to pull it, then I wasn't, then the uncertainty of just standing there was worse than anything else could ever be, and I reached out and tugged it.

Just when I was hoping she wouldn't answer, she appeared. I was scared that it showed in my face that I didn't belong in a house and that she would kick me out or never even let me in.

"Buenos días. Did you leave something here?" she said.

I didn't answer her, because I knew I hadn't left anything and by her face I knew that was the only right reason why I could have come. I turned, ready to run.

"M'hija, stop!" she called. "Come back! Come in!"

I went back. She led me past the room where Uncle and I had been, farther down the corridor to an outdoor patio with a purple fuchsia tree, old wooden chairs, and a wooden table with wet blossoms stuck to it. She brushed off the table and the chairs with a cloth, and we sat down.

She asked me my name, and I told her Tzunún.

She said I didn't have to call her señora, that I could call her Doña Celestina.

She asked if Baltasar Om was any kind of relative at all.

"I call him Uncle," I said softly, "but he isn't my uncle, not really."

"I thought not," she said. "You don't know if he was at La Hortensia years ago?"

"He's never mentioned it. I don't know."

"Of course you wouldn't know," Doña Celestina said. "The evil that went on up there happened before you were born."

I asked her what La Hortensia was.

She said twenty years before it had been a big plantation, where a lot of poor Mayan families worked for one rich ladino for hardly any money, taking care of cattle and picking coffee. At that time a lot of people, some ladinos, too, were fighting to change the government, because it just served the rich, and some of the men on the farm were secretly guerrilla fighters against the army.

They convinced all the poor families to strike and demand higher wages.

The rich ladino who owned the farm found out that the poor workers were striking—not taking care of any of his cattle or picking any of his coffee. He called friends, who happened to be generals in the army, and said his workers wanted to overthrow the government.

The soldiers came at break of day. They shot the men, the women, and all the children, too. By noon they had killed everyone. Then they cut down young trees and turned them into stakes pointed on both ends.

They ran the stakes through the dead bodies the way the vendors at fairs run toothpicks through tacos. The soldiers would push a stake through a dead man, a dead woman, a dead child or two, another murdered man. As many bodies as would fit. Once they had them all on stakes, they piled them up and burned them.

All the people who worked or lived at La Hortensia. And one more, because Doña Celestina's husband had been there, too, that very morning, visiting a friend. He didn't work there; he hadn't done anything against the government. The soldiers killed him just because they were killing everybody, and he would have been a witness to the murders if he'd lived.

"I ask myself why there wasn't a sign," Doña Celestina said, "why I got no warning from the ancestors or the Ahau or the little seeds. Unless I missed a sign. Unless there was a sign that I ignored, something I should have noticed that I didn't. I asked the seeds time and time again if I overlooked a warning, and they always told me no. But why it had to happen I'll never understand."

She let out a long breath.

"About noon that day I went to look for my husband," Doña Celestina said. "When I got near La Hortensia, soldiers passed me on an army truck, and then I saw the black smoke billowing, rolling into the sky—terrible smoke that smelled of human flesh.

"I never saw my husband again, not even his body. For fear of the army, nobody dared to go bury the dead, not for a long time."

The pain in her eyes started far back, and the more I looked into her eyes the farther back the pain went and the deeper it became, until I knew there was no end to it and I thought it was something I had no right to see.

Her hands opened on the table, cupped as if they yearned to hold something. On the ground under the fuchsia tree, a fallen purple blossom lay, the outer petals holding the inner ones like a cradle. I picked it up and set it in her hands. Tears gathered in her eyes.

"Armando," she said softly. "Armando was his name.

"I never talk about La Hortensia to anyone," she said.

"I don't know why I'm telling all this to someone young as you."

I wanted to say something, but I didn't know what, so I said nothing.

Doña Celestina kissed the purple flower and rested it gently on the table. "After what I saw that day, I ask myself how I can still be living. But here I am."

She raised her head. "I wasn't well disposed to your so-called uncle, thinking I saw him coming from La Hortensia. —Why have you come to see me?"

I liked you, I thought, but I couldn't say that. That wasn't enough of a reason to see a person. To just go to a stranger's house because you liked her.

"I don't know."

"You probably have a reason, Tzunún, whether you know it or not. Sometimes the reasons we don't know are the most important ones—the ones that should guide us. But tell me your whole name."

"Tzunún Chumil," I said shyly. Hummingbird Star.

"Tzunún Chumil, it's a pleasure to know you," she said. "Will you share breakfast with me?"

I nodded yes.

"Will you help me get it ready?"

We went into her kitchen. In an enamel pot over the fire, there was boiled coffee ready. She asked me to get the cups and pour it, and stir sugar in, as much as I wanted in mine, just two spoonfuls in hers.

She scrambled eggs, and I ladled out black beans from a clay pot over the fire. She had tortillas that we heated till they were crisp and curling at the edges. I wrapped them in a yellow cloth. Doña Celestina shared the eggs out just even, one plate for her, one for me. We took everything out to the patio.

"Tzunún, I thank you for the work you've done to feed us," Doña Celestina said, and I remembered how to answer, the way I'd done when I was little.

"Doña Celestina, I thank you for the work you've done to feed us."

10

Doña Celestina Heals Me

"S-s-s-sometimes I wonder if I have a snake in my throat. Or a devil."

I hadn't meant to tell her; the words just came out.

"I'll see." She put her hand on my forehead. "Tip your head back. Open your mouth."

I opened my mouth as wide as I could, and she looked in. Then she felt my throat under my jaw where the problem came from.

"All fine," she said. "No snake. No devil."

I let out a heavy breath. I was glad but I was sorry, too. Because if it wasn't a devil, then it was my fault. My fault for being stupid.

She put her arm around my shoulders and spoke as if she read my mind. "It's not your fault," she said, "and you're not stupid, either. Do you know how I can be sure of that?"

I shook my head.

"The stupid have no problem talking, that's why. They can talk all day and all night, just like the birds. Yours is a problem of the intelligent. You want to talk, but you're afraid of things you need to say. Afraid of the consequences of saying those things. Isn't that right?"

What she said sounded true, and yet I didn't know what it was I had to say, what it was I couldn't.

"It's all right to be silent," she said. "But from now on, when you say what you need to say, it is going to get easier. Tonight I'll do a special blessing for your words. I'll ask your words to be good to you. So from tomorrow on, they'll be your friends.

"And you, too, can tell the words you know they're friends, that you know they want to help you."

I nodded again. I touched my throat. No snake. No devil. I didn't even feel a lump there.

"Hummingbirds are a sign of peace. They announce great blessings," Doña Celestina said. "I like your name. I'd like to hear you say it loud."

"Tzunún Chumil!" I said. My voice shocked me, so loud it seemed as if everybody in Nebaj must hear me. But I guess it wasn't so loud after all, because Doña Celestina only smiled.

"Your nickname is Colibrí, isn't it?" she said.

"Yes, it's the name my mother called me."

"I thought so," Doña Celestina said. "And it's a beautiful name, too. Say it loudly!"

I did.

"—Why does Baltasar say your name is Rosa Garcia?"

"I don't know. He told me long ago that 'Rosa Garcia' is easier to pronounce."

"There is something strange about your past," Doña Celestina said. "Something deeply hidden. I wish I could find the secret."

"Uncle says my parents probably didn't want me. They lost me on purpose, he says."

"That's not true," Doña Celestina said. "I'm sure. I can feel that they wanted you. Only what exactly happened, I can't sense." She paused, as if she was listening for something being said just beyond her hearing, and then gave up.

"One thing, Baltasar was wrong to take your name away from you. If he had to change something, he should have changed his own name. 'Om' means 'Spider,' and it's a bad last name."

"Why?" I said.

Celestina shrugged. "A visit from a spider is no good. But to see a colibrí is very lucky."

"Once," I told her, "I was sitting by a road alone, waiting for Uncle, all by myself and so lonely, and one flew down and hovered right in front of my face. I had flowers in my hands, but it didn't touch the flowers, it just stared at me for the longest time. Like a friend. Like my best friend."

"It made you a gift of itself," Doña Celestina said. "That doesn't happen often. Don't forget it. Don't forget the things that mean most to you. They're more valuable than gold."

Doña Celestina ran a finger carefully around the rim of her coffee cup, as if it were a road she was tracing.

"Have you ever thought of leaving Baltasar?"

"How can I leave him, when I have to find him a treasure? Even you say so."

"Don't worry about the treasure," she said. "What's going to happen will happen. Even if you left him, that wouldn't change."

"He takes care of me," I said.

Doña Celestina hesitated, choosing her words carefully. "Respect is the basis of life, Tzunún. And it's a duty for a child to be loyal to the person who cares for her. But sometimes that person isn't good. Are you sure Baltasar is good for you, Tzunún?"

"When I was left, he found me on the street. He rescued me."

"And since then, where have you and he lived?"

"Everywhere, seems like."

"What do you do?"

I could say it, but I felt a lump in my throat all the same. "We beg."

Doña Celestina warmed her hands against her coffee cup. "You could have a better life," she said. "You wouldn't need to beg. I know a place in the capital where you could go, a place where you could go to school and live with other children."

She explained a little more, but I told her no.

The place she was talking about is called an orphanage. A place for children who don't have anybody. I didn't want to be where everybody was together but nobody belonged to anybody.

"So no matter what, you don't want to leave Baltasar?" she said, and just the idea of leaving him frightened me so much that at first I couldn't think.

11

Split

"No," I said, "I don't want to leave him," but even when I said it, I didn't know if I was right, and I felt something in my heart was winding up inside me tighter and tighter like a rubber band that would finally break.

"If . . ."

"Continue, child, what is it you want to say?"

"If I c-c-could live with you . . ." I said, but when I looked at her face, my words trailed off, because I could see the answer was no. I bit my lips to keep from crying. I stood up and gathered my shawl.

She reached out and held my hand.

"That's something very big you're asking for," she said gently. "I would like to have you stay with me, but I can't."

"Why not?" My shoulders were shaking. She pulled me down into a chair and put her arm around me.

"It would be a mess."

I tried to get up, but she held me.

"I'll tell you why," she said. "Then you tell me if I'm wrong."

So she explained. She said if she kept me, Uncle would find out where I was, and he'd want me because of the treasure, if for no other reason, though maybe he even loved me, too, in his way.

Anyhow, he'd want to get me back, she said, and he'd come looking for me.

"Tzunún, then you might just go with him because you wanted to—"

I shook my head furiously to deny it, to tell her I wouldn't leave her.

"—which you might do—I don't believe your denial—and I would be unhappy, but it would be your right, your choice."

"I wouldn't go," I said softly.

Doña Celestina's arms dropped from around me, but she kept her eyes on mine.

"And that's where the mess would begin. Baltasar could go to the police and say I'd kidnapped you, and even if he isn't your relative, the court would take his word, because you've been with him so long."

She straightened out my clenched fingers and rubbed them with hers.

"Yes, eventually it would come to that," she said, "the police would be here, and then everything would depend on your word. —Do you understand?"

"No." I didn't want to understand.

"You mean 'yes,' Doña Celestina said, "because you do understand. —What would you say if you stayed with me and Baltasar came and wanted you back?"

I didn't know. I tried to imagine it, me living at her house, which was an impossible paradise, and Uncle returning and saying, "Come on, Rosa. I'm here. It's time to go. We have to go."

In my head I could already hear him saying those words.

I couldn't hear what I would say back.

I was so used to him. I was used to being quiet when he wanted me to be quiet. I was used to doing what he said. Whenever he told me to pack to get ready to go, I packed and got ready. That was the way we lived.

Doña Celestina shook her head. "If you didn't say anything, your silence would mean: 'Yes, Uncle, I'm going with you.' I'd lose you, just when I was getting to know you.

"And not only that—I might be fined, or have to go to jail, if you wouldn't speak up for me. —Don't you see, Tzunún? I can't take you! I don't dare!"

She watched me, her face half angry, half sad. "Do you understand?"

I understood, but I didn't answer, just took hold of my coffee cup, as if to take it to the kitchen, but didn't stand, only my knees trembled, my shoulders trembled, and the cup trembled, too.

Doña Celestina took the cup from me and set it back on the table. I took a long breath. "He's told me I can leave him if I want to."

"That's the question," Doña Celestina said. "The question is if you really want to." She sat down beside me.

"If I stayed here with you right this minute, if I just never went back . . ."

"He would come here looking for you, you know."

I nodded. I knew.

"It's not that I don't want you, Tzunún. It's that *you* don't know what you want. Your heart's divided."

Divided! Divided meant split. I had a split heart, and my road would be split as well—part of me going ahead, part of me always looking back. Looking back toward Doña Celestina, toward this very minute when I was losing her.

"You came here for something more," Doña Celestina said. "I feel it. What is it?"

I started to say she was wrong, and then I remembered my notebook. I took it out of my shawl.

"Uncle said you're right that he owes me a little paper, and he bought this for me."

"That was good of him," Doña Celestina said, and then hesitated. She asked to hold the notebook.

I passed it to her. She held it with her eyes closed. I watched and didn't make a sound.

She opened her eyes and returned it.

"Tzunún," she said, "the ancestors talk to me, so believe what I say, it's important. This isn't the paper Baltasar owes you. The paper he owes you is something else.

"—Just one sheet, really small," she added. "About this size . . ." She traced a square that covered the palm of my hand.

"So he gave me extra," I said.

"Yes, but he still owes you that one sheet. It has something written on it. I don't know why, but the ancestors tell me you must find it."

"All right, I'll ask Uncle for it," I said.

"No," Doña Celestina said, "don't! If you ask about it, he'll destroy it! Try to find it on your own. Secretly. —And you need to go now; surely he'll be looking for you."

She walked me to the gate, put her hand on my head, and spoke quickly in Ixil. Of all she said, I understood only my name. The whole thing sounded like a prayer, though. A blessing.

"Take this, too," she said. "It's yours." She pulled a little purse from her huipil and handed me a perfect, brand-new hundred-quetzal bill.

I didn't ask her how she knew. I didn't wonder, I didn't even thank her. I just put my arms around her, and she put her arms around me. I loved her, loved her so much I felt my heart would burst.

She broke the circle of my arms and held my hands in hers.

"You're a fine girl, Tzunún. Don't let anybody tell you

different. When you get in trouble, think of your treasures. Think of the hummingbird that visited you on the road. Think of our time together. The real treasures lead the way out of darkness."

"And Uncle? His treasure?"

"A treasure depends on who sees it," was all she said.

12

Uncle's Plan

On the way to the church, I kept feeling my throat to see if it was truly healed. It really seemed to be—all smooth, with no lump in it.

The lump had moved. It was in my heart.

I told myself I'd go back to Doña Celestina's another day and ask her to cure my heart the way she'd cured my throat. At the church, I'd look for the man with the beautiful hat, and I'd talk to him longer and find out his name, and maybe he'd be my friend.

But somehow, even before I saw Uncle, I knew these things would not happen. And then there I was at the church, and right where I'd left him, there was Uncle, sitting cross-legged under the portico, with the rope bag around the old black suitcase and the walking stick by his side, his whole body filled with impatience, and his eyes on the distant mountains.

I'd bought him food on the way. I handed him two tortillas with scrambled eggs rolled inside them.

"Why are you so late?"

"By chance I saw the Day-Keeper. She talked to me awhile."

"Awhile! Hours," Uncle grunted. But he didn't ask me any more about Doña Celestina, just occupied himself with eating, and then he told me we were leaving.

He lifted the suitcase onto his back and passed me the end of his stick. We started walking, me in front, him grumbling at my back.

He said he didn't like Nebaj. He didn't like the rain. Besides, he had found out that in Ixil, the word "Nebaj" means "poor." In a five-centavo town like that, I'd never make him rich.

He took long steps, and I had to hurry to stay ahead of him. I thought we'd be walking for days, crossing the mountains, but instead we went only to the telephone company office. Uncle was going to call his old friend Raimundo—the one he had owed money for so long.

He sat down inside the glass booth. I hoped the operator wouldn't get the call through, hoped Uncle would hang up the phone right away and come out saying he couldn't find his friend anywhere, the trip was off, and after all, Nebaj was a good place to stay.

Uncle leaned back in the booth. I saw his lips moving, saw him gesturing, showing five fingers and an empty palm, then nodding, first once, then eagerly, many times.

He came out smiling. He had a whole new plan for us. We were going to Raimundo's town, San Sebastián. Uncle could make a lot of money there, Raimundo said, and so could I. We wouldn't need to beg. We could work together, Uncle and Raimundo and me, all three of us partners, and Uncle could pay Raimundo back his debt and live well.

And we weren't going to walk across the mountains. Not at all. Raimundo needed us fast. We were going right away, on the bus, and when we got there, Raimundo would even pay Uncle back for the bus tickets, no problem.

13

On the Road

The bus was striped pink, purple, and light green, and it gleamed in the rain. The helper climbed onto the roof and roped down our old black suitcase alongside other bags and baskets, covering everything under long sheets of plastic.

Water dripped off our blue plastic rain sheets. The doors of the bus opened, and Uncle pinched me to make me climb in.

The driver started the engine. It sounded like a corn-grinding mill mashing every kernel to bits.

People crowded in behind Uncle and me, pushing us down the aisle toward the back. The metal roof crunched under the helper's footsteps, rang with thuds and banging.

Uncle pressed me into a narrow row of seats, pressing me farther in till I was shoved up against the window.

The bus was full. It smelled of woodsmoke and the spit-up milk of babies and wet clothes and tortillas carried for the journey. Parents and grandparents held babies in their laps, while older kids stood in the aisles, clinging to the backs of seats.

Around us some passengers were trying to open the windows, because there was no air. Others were trying to close them because of the rain, and those who couldn't get to the windows themselves were muttering about the re-arrangements.

"See how lucky you are?" Uncle said. "Traveling on a bus! And you got a seat!"

Out the window I saw a boy selling purple and orange sodas in plastic bags.

"Want some pop?" Uncle said. "Want some lunch?"

I shook my head. A sick feeling started up in my insides and spread all through me. I had to get off that bus. Had to.

I stood up. Uncle blocked my way, stretching out his arms to the top of the seat in front of us. "Sit down, Rosa! Where do you think you're going? I paid! We can't get our money back!"

I shook my head and stayed standing. Uncle put his arms around my waist and pulled me down.

"There's no sense to you, Rosa! You want to walk in the rain for days? Sit down!"

I sat, curling myself against the hard seat, swallowing, trying to drive the bad feeling down into the pit of my stomach.

The bus lurched forward, swaying along the uneven street. I wiped the steam off the window to see Nebaj one last time, but it did no good—rain was running heavily now down the outside of the glass. All I could see was a wavering blur of pale buildings, then the unending watery green of mountains.

I shut my eyes tight. A baby cried. Someone shushed it, but it kept wailing.

I was losing something, something more than just Nebaj. Inside my head I pronounced my own name. Tzunún Chumil. Tzunún Chumil. Tzunún Chumil. And then my nickname. Colibrí, I said, over and over to myself. The word turned into a vision of my mother, her voice. The look of her, her prettiness. The memory of the house where I used to live.

We had land with blue morning glories clinging to the fence and hollyhocks all along the edges of the yard.

In the yard my father would hold me by the hands and fly me, swinging me around and around, and I'd see the hollyhocks rushing past me.

I loved it when my dad flew me. I wanted to fly for real—fly like the hummingbirds darting between the blossoms, speeding like them, hovering like them.

If I got close enough to them and wished, I could make it happen.

A tiny hummingbird buzzed by my ear, then dove into a morning glory blossom by the gate. I climbed the gate to touch it, leaned out toward it, close and closer still, so close my cheek could feel the breeze from its wings. *I want to be . . .* I wished. I reached, I fell.

The hummingbird rocketed through sky.

How could I have fallen? Colibrí was my name. But colibrís don't fall, ever. I sobbed from grief—grief I was no hummingbird.

My mother ran to me, held me. She kissed my forehead and stroked my knees to take the pain away. She rubbed the top of my head on that special place where if you touch it, it makes a baby peaceful.

"Tzunún," she said, "you're all right! My sweet child, my darling Colibrí."

On the bus, the baby no longer cried. Some people were asleep. Some talked quietly, two were talking loudly, showing off, using the new kind of phones people call *celulares*.

Uncle leaned forward, his thick hands braced against the seat in front of us, his head nodding, perfectly calm. But horror was in me, the sickness worse than motion sickness, a dread as if I were spinning down and down into nothingness.

In my mind another trip had started, one I was living again: a bus trip I'd made, when I was very small, to the capital, Guatemala City, with my parents.

We were on a city bus, starting on the way home. I stood in the aisle in front of my mother, pressing my face into the softness of her belly, holding on to her belt. My father leaned against the wall of the bus, holding a box of things we'd bought.

The back door was open all the time, and even when the bus was moving, people would jump off. Through the door I could see buildings with big glass windows and pale walls streaked with soot.

"You can look, Colibrí, but hang on to me tight!" my mother said.

The bus stopped. Some people got out, and one man jumped on. He stood right in front of me and stared at me. His face was dirty and his eyes shone red like lit coals. "Mamá," I said and held tighter to her belt, but he grabbed my arms and jerked and I couldn't hold on anymore, I was over his shoulder, screaming and kicking as hard as I could. My father dropped the box, yelling, and sprang toward us. Other passengers were shouting "Kidnapper! Stop the bus!" But then I didn't hear them anymore because the strange man was running through a crowd with me, and some people stared and some reached out to slow him down because I was still screaming, but he told them, "A bee stung my daughter," and kept running. I shouted "No!" over and over but he went so fast they didn't listen to me.

In an alley he covered my nose and mouth with a bad-smelling cloth that made me choke. I woke up there all alone.

Leaving Nebaj, I shut my eyes, trying to see into the past, to the face of the man who took me. I stared into memory, but memory stung like a well of poisoned tears, blinding me, and in the end all I could remember was Uncle.

He found me that day in the alley. He asked me what was wrong and said he'd take care of me.

When I was older and could understand more, he told me how, after I told him my name, he talked with the police and read all the newspapers, looking for who had lost Tzunún Chumil, but there was no news. Maybe my parents had taken me to the capital to lose me on purpose, for lack of money to keep me. It happens, he said.

He told me his opinion so many times that everything I'd seen and felt that day got mixed up with the things he said, and at last it seemed as if I had parents who didn't want to get me back.

But I dreamed about them often. Sometimes I had a dream that we were together on a bus, and they turned away from me because I did something very bad. In the dream I would try to remember what I'd done, so I could ask them for forgiveness, because I knew if I only asked, everything would be all right. But no matter how hard I tried to remember, I never could. And all the while I was trying, the bus was stretching out, getting longer and longer, so long that finally, though the three of us were still on the same bus together, the space between me and my parents was so great I couldn't even see them, and there was no hope we would ever be close again.

That was a terrible dream, and it was exactly the same every time I had it. It agreed with what Uncle said, so I always thought there was truth in it. I'd done something bad, so my parents didn't want me. I'd believed that practically forever. But Doña Celestina said it wasn't so. Uncle helped me and took care of me. But that didn't make him always right. About my parents, he was mistaken.

14

My Cup

Uncle shook me by the shoulder, told me to wake up. We had to change buses. We were in the town of Sacapulas, and we'd have an hour to wait for the bus to San Sebastián.

A giant ceiba tree with enormous branches shaded the street and the park next to it. The helper handed down our suitcase, and we walked to a food stand where a woman sold us little tamales mixed with a delicious green herb, chipilín.

Uncle ordered himself a Coca-Cola and I ordered hot chocolate. We sat on a park bench and ate. Uncle finished and went off across the street. He bought a newspaper and started talking to some men. He was on vacation— wearing his good pants and not begging or pretending to be blind.

I sat alone on the bench. I was still waiting for my hot chocolate.

Just the way it always was when we left somewhere, the place and the people left behind stopped being real for me. Nebaj seemed pale and blurry, and Doña Celestina was just another person, a nice person but long gone.

At the food stand the woman was beating my chocolate with a wooden beater. I could see the foam on the top of it.

She reached to a shelf and took down a cup with a design of hearts—one big red perfect heart, with a green vine spinning from it that grew three tiny hearts.

The big heart put me in mind of how Doña Celestina said she couldn't keep me because of my divided heart. When she said it I'd believed it, but now I wasn't sure. Maybe she hadn't wanted me, anyway. Maybe she was wrong, and there wasn't any little piece of paper that Uncle owed me. Maybe I didn't even have a divided heart. And why should I try to do what she said about remembering things that had mattered when I couldn't be sure that they mattered at all?

The woman poured my chocolate and smiled at me, and somehow that made me angry, as if the woman were Doña Celestina herself. Inside I was shouting at Doña Celestina, *"I don't have a divided heart!"*

I picked up the hot chocolate. The cup exploded. It fell apart in my hand, and I jumped. Chocolate streamed all over the counter. The cup lay in the middle of the mess, split in two. The break passed through the biggest red heart—divided it right down the middle.

The woman wiped up the spill. "I should have known that cup would go!" she said. "It had a crack starting."

She thought it was just natural, but to me it was a sign. I had a divided heart, just as Doña Celestina said. Just as she had told me, that was why she wouldn't keep me. That and no other reason. Not because I would have cost her too much or she didn't like me.

"Patience, girl, there's more in the pitcher," the woman said. She poured chocolate into a plain white mug and handed it to me.

She picked up the two pieces of the broken cup. "Into the trash with you!" she said. My heart almost stopped, because I thought maybe her words were another sign, and it was I of the split heart who was really going into the garbage.

I begged her for the pieces.

She looked surprised, then shrugged. "Well, after all, they're no use to me."

She rinsed them off in a bucket of water, dried them, and handed them to me wrapped in a sheet of old newspaper.

"Maybe you can join the pieces with a little glue," she said.

I wrapped them in my shawl.

The next bus came, the one to San Sebastián, painted with orange-and-blue stripes and a design of red diamonds. Uncle and I jumped on, and once more he shoved me into a seat against a window.

We left Santa Cruz. Uncle stared out the window, looking over my head at a ravine where lots of people had thrown trash, and beyond it to where some goats were eating.

I was glad he didn't know I was carrying a broken cup. If he knew, he'd say I should throw it out the window to join the other garbage, that I was crazy to carry it around—two fragile pieces of pottery that would smash into a jillion more at the first knock.

He coughed once, then closed his eyes.

I opened my shawl and put the two pieces of the cup together. They fit perfectly. From the big heart, the green vine wound around the cup growing the three small hearts. It had been—it still could be—a beautiful cup.

Uncle always said beauty was nothing but an idea stupid sheep and idiot fools believed in. A broken cup not even fit to trick a fool, that's what he'd say I had.

But it was mine.

Until Uncle got me the notebook, all my life with him I had never had anything really my own—and even the notebook was only his idea because Doña Celestina said he owed me paper. It was nothing I had chosen completely by myself.

I put the pieces of the cup back in my shawl, touching them through the cloth.

A person can't live without something beautiful. Even

if it was just something another person would have put in the trash, I had my cup, and to me it was beautiful.

We passed down into a valley, through a banana plantation. On long chain-like stalks, buds hung down full and heavy, dark purple-red, the size of human hearts. Higher up, frayed green branches tossed, banana leaves split by the wind. Split, but living still.

15

San Sebastián

The road was cut into the edge of a mountain. Below, a huge lake glittered in the sunset. Behind it, above a wall of violet clouds, three volcanoes seemed to be floating in the sky.

"Five minutes more, maybe ten, we'll be there," Uncle said. "And it's a rich town. A lot of foreigners visit it and pay to see the beauty. Fools that they are."

The bus inched downward, the driver braking and keeping it slow so it didn't fly off a cliff. The road turned flat, and wider, and suddenly there was a forest of painted signs bunched along the side of the highway and a big gas station where the driver turned in, shouting, "San Sebastián, San Sebastián!"

Everybody got out. The helper passed down Uncle's suitcase from the roof.

On the other side of the street a big silver bus was parked in front of a fancy two-story hotel painted turquoise and gold. By the entrance stood a huge steel statue of a soldier on a horse, carrying a shield and a spear.

Uncle frowned.

"Drooling imbeciles, they made the Conquistador Pedro de Alvarado wrong. He should have a gun. The Conquistadors came with guns. That's how they won."

He looked at the silver bus, so much bigger and nicer than the one we'd been on.

"Tourists ride special," Uncle said. "The better to gawk at things. Buzzards that they are."

Led by a ragged boy, a man crawled down the sidewalk toward the silver bus, his legs covered with thick leather pads that stuck out on both sides of his knees like doormats. He had a big cardboard sign on a cord around his neck, with a drawing on it—two eyes with bristly curly lashes that had big X's over them. Blind, that's what the sign claimed.

He crawled in front of the statue and stopped, holding his hands up toward the windows of the silver bus.

Maybe he was blind, but there was nothing wrong with his legs or his feet. I could see that.

From the silver bus, a bunch of people dropped a shower of silver coins.

The ragged boy ran to pick up the money.

The beggar stayed still. His hands and his head never moved.

"A true professional," Uncle said.

What if Raimundo didn't really have jobs for us? What if Uncle got himself some kneepads, too, and crawled all around the streets of San Sebastián? What if I had to lead him? I didn't think I could stand it.

The silver bus started up, blue smoke rolling out of the tailpipe, and turned onto the highway.

Still holding up his empty palms, the man with the kneepads looked at the statue of the Conquistador. The Conquistador didn't drop him a centavo.

The streetlights of San Sebastián lit up—fancy ones with iron posts and round white lights that looked like clusters of pearls. In their purplish glow, a man ran toward Uncle, hugged him, and laughed with pleasure. Uncle set down the suitcase and hugged him back.

"Baltasar, old buddy! How's everything?"

" 'Mundo!" Uncle said.

They broke apart, smiling at each other.

Girls aren't supposed to stare at men, but it was hard not to stare at Raimundo. He had a bright face shaped like an owl's, light skin, silvery hair in a crew cut that came down a little on his forehead in a peak, and very round, innocent-looking eyes.

He wore pressed black jeans, a black leather jacket, shiny black cowboy boots. His hat was special, too—a black felt cowboy hat with silver rivets in the band. He looked so much better than Uncle there was no comparison.

He put his arm around my shoulder and gave me a kiss on the cheek. "Very pretty, Rosa, you're a young lady now!"

He must have seen me when I was little, but I didn't remember him.

"Rosa's still a kid," Uncle said.

"Not so, no more!" Raimundo was very merry about my growing up.

Uncle examined me. "Maybe she's thirteen. I should give her more to carry."

Raimundo glanced around, saw the beggar with the kneepads on the other side of the street, and made a face.

"No use wasting time here," he said; "let's go. —I've got my own place now."

He picked up Uncle's suitcase.

"You don't need to carry it," Uncle said. "Rosa can do it."

"No problem," Raimundo said.

We started walking, Raimundo swinging the old suitcase in the rope bag as if it were light.

"You're not at your sister's anymore?" Uncle said.

"No more. She has face problems."

"I remember Dolores as good-looking," Uncle said. "Stuck up, though."

"Yeah, well—but she has problems. Long tongue. Long nose."

Long tongue—somebody who tells things she has no business telling. Long nose—somebody who sticks her nose into other people's business.

"She should watch out," Raimundo said. "She might lose her nose one day." He swung the suitcase harder, so high it hit a boy in front of us right in the middle of his back.

"Sorry, brother," Raimundo said.

It was near seven, and in most towns the streets would have been almost dark. Not in San Sebastián. The streetlights had it lit up like a fair.

Big stores were still open, and they had lights, too, shining down on all the stuff behind glass windows.

We passed one store with beds and bicycles and TVs and strange white metal boxes that Raimundo told me washed clothes. I couldn't see how.

Uncle and Raimundo were talking like mad, but I didn't listen. There was so much to see. Fancy cars on the street, not just pickups. Foreigners on the sidewalks speaking strange languages. Some old ones with packages and canes, young ones who looked like giants, carrying huge backpacks.

We passed by a restaurant that had lots of foreigners inside dressed in fancy clothes. One woman wore a very tight dress that looked like it was made of gold. A waiter in black pants and a white shirt with ruffles poured red sauce from a silver dish over her ice cream. He lit a match and blue flames flared up. Ice cream on fire! I couldn't believe it.

We passed a school. Teenage boys and girls, all with backpacks and wearing blue sweaters, were going in to study, even though it was nighttime. In a lot of towns, school is just for little kids and that's all.

"They work in the day, they study at night," Raimundo said.

We turned down a paved walking street. There were no fancy lampposts on it, just plain ones. High above the street the lacy branches of jacaranda trees caught the light, and the paving shone a bright purple-blue with their fallen flowers.

We passed small houses with fenced yards and got to a faded pink concrete-block house with a padlocked wire gate. Raimundo took out a key.

"Yours?" Uncle tried to hide it, but I could tell he was amazed that Raimundo had a house.

The padlock flew open.

"Mine," Raimundo said.

16

Tango

In the main room of Raimundo's house, there were four chairs and a table, two beds against a side wall, and a wooden cupboard with warped doors with a tape player and tapes on top of it. Over the door we'd come in, there was a big bunch of garlic wrapped in red cellophane, to keep evil out.

Raimundo gestured at the beds. "You and I sleep here," he told Uncle.

He opened the inner door to a short corridor with two rooms off it, a bathroom and the room that was going to be mine.

That room had three straw mats piled up on the floor under a window.

"Rosa, you can sleep there," Raimundo said.

I looked at the mats and said they were nice and set the things in my shawl down by them.

Across the room, there were some decorations on the wall and a table with a white cloth and a black candle burning.

"It's an altar," Raimundo said. "Go look if you want."

I walked over to it, Uncle close behind me. The black candle was burning inside a tall thick glass. Above it, six U.S. dollar bills were tacked to the wall, around a big poster of a skinny man dressed in a red, white, and blue suit and a tall hat, who was pointing one bony finger at the world. Along the edge of the table there were five cigars, and a basket with balls of spicy copal incense.

Uncle pointed to the cigars. "You smoke?"

"The saint and I share a few," Raimundo said.

"What saint is he?" I asked. I didn't know if I wanted to sleep in that room, with that holy man glaring down on me and pointing.

"Saint Sam," Raimundo said. "I talk to him morning and night. You'll have to stay out of here then, sorry. Also, that candle in front of him must stay lit all the time, day and night. If you mess with it, I'll cut off your nose."

I could tell he didn't mean it. At least, I thought I could.

"I won't touch it," I said.

Uncle asked Raimundo how come Saint Sam was his saint.

He said choosing a personal saint was an individual thing, you knew from your dreams when you needed a saint and which one, but it was something you shouldn't talk about much. But he could say that Sam was an uncle, and the principal saint of the U.S.A., and the U.S.A. was the richest country in the world, so Saint Sam had to be powerful and good at making people rich. He had tacked up the dollar bills around him so that Saint Sam wouldn't get absentminded and forget what he was supposed to give in return for all the attention he was getting.

Uncle said for his part he didn't believe in the Christian saints, but that a lot of people used San Simón Judas as the one to ask for money.

"Him?" Raimundo said. "In life he sold Jesus for thirty pieces of silver—so the people who pray to him think he'll do anything, that he has no limits. They forget he hanged himself after."

"I didn't know," Uncle said, frowning. I could tell he was regretting the candles he'd lit to San Simón Judas.

We went out to the main room. Raimundo said he had dinner for us and lifted a cloth that draped pots on the table. Underneath there were beans and rice, still warm; open-faced tacos with lettuce, beets, tuna, and hard-boiled eggs; and a big pitcher of papaya drink.

"Where'd this come from?" Uncle asked.

Raimundo brought plates and glasses from the cupboard. "Dolores. I pay her. She brings the food over every day."

It was all delicious, and there was plenty.

Afterward I washed the dishes at a small pila in the backyard. Raimundo switched on an outside light so I could see.

When I brought the clean dishes in, there were Coke and rum and glasses out on the table, and Uncle was cutting some limes.

Raimundo asked me if I liked rum. I said I didn't know.

"One way to find out! Ladies first!" Raimundo put his hand on my glass, but Uncle stopped him.

"Rosa's too young."

"Too young? A pretty girl like that? She's almost old enough to get married!"

"She can't marry till she's fourteen," Uncle said.

"I don't want to get married, anyhow," I said.

"You would if you could marry me," Raimundo bragged, and grinned. He poured me some plain Coca-Cola with a flourish.

He was trying to gain territory. That's what girls call it when a man boasts about how great he is. Nobody ever acted that way with me before. It was interesting but it scared me. "R-R-Raimundo," I said, "I wouldn't want to marry you; you're too old."

Raimundo laughed as if I'd made a great joke. Uncle smirked. "You see?" he said triumphantly.

Raimundo waved a hand, brushing away Uncle's words and mine, too. He poured some more Coca-Cola in my glass, and rum and Coke into his and Uncle's.

He made a toast to the three of us, because we were partners. "One for all and all for one," he said, and we clinked glasses.

Raimundo and Uncle sipped their drinks, every now and then squeezing in some lime. I drank my Coke.

Raimundo asked me if I liked music.

I said yes, even though I knew it might make Uncle mad. Uncle always said music was for sheep.

Raimundo said he'd play a special tape just for me—music from Argentina.

I asked him what town Argentina was, and he said it wasn't a town, it was a country way south of here, the last country before the South Pole, where the world turns to ice. At least, he claimed that down south the world turns to ice, but whenever he looked serious I thought maybe he was fooling.

"What you'll be hearing is accordion music, my dear Rosa," he said. "It's music made by a folding box the musician squeezes."

How could a folding box make music? I didn't ask.

Raimundo popped a tape into the player, and the music began, with a strange starting-and-stopping rhythm I'd never heard before—flowing toward happiness and then colliding with disaster, skidding into sadness, but then turning around somehow, back toward hope.

Sometimes there were words, and the words were about people and places that the singer had loved and was going to miss forever, but maybe find again—that was where the hope came in. The music made me think of my parents, and how I always, always hoped I'd find them, even though it seemed as if there was no chance.

"These songs are tangos," Raimundo said.

I liked the word. Tangos.

All the music I usually heard was marimba music, the popular music in Guatemala. In marimba all the notes seem to say, "Be happy and cheerful, everything is fine, and what isn't it's wiser to forget."

Tango had a different voice. It didn't say everything was fine, it mixed up hope and pain and love and regret until you didn't even know which was which. It made me feel all those things. Feel too much. And yet I wanted to hear it forever.

"Dance with me!" Raimundo said. And before I could say no, he had me by the shoulders and out of my chair.

"I never danced with anybody!" I said. "I don't know how."

"I'll teach you," Raimundo said. He pulled me into the middle of the room.

"Your feet follow my feet. Three steps backward and then *bend*!" he said. He wanted me to arch backward, but I didn't.

"You're light as a feather, but you have a body like lead. Like a tree trunk! That's impossible, it can't be!

We'll try it again. I'll walk you backward. One two *three*! You can't fall, I'm holding you, lean back!"

His hand was around my waist. I leaned against it.

"Good! And now we'll go forward and—whirl!"

In a way I felt like I did when I was little, when my father whirled me across the yard, except this felt stranger and more dangerous.

"Now forward!"

I thought forward would be easier, but it was harder, because I had to take fast running steps without running into Raimundo's feet.

Raimundo told Uncle that I really ought to have rum, just a little bit, so I'd relax, but Uncle said no.

We stood in the middle of the floor. "Just forget everything and feel the music," Raimundo said, and I felt the swirl of it.

"Now then," Raimundo said, "forget that you're a girl. Forget that I'm a man. We aren't that anymore. I'm the wind, and you're a leaf. You can spin, you can fly, you're a leaf.

"Go forward, one two three, you're a leaf not a tree trunk. Bend." And I bent, and it felt right, magical, and I was dancing. Dancing the tango, caught in the sudden stops and whirls of it, the swing of it, the shocking almost falls of it, and caught in Raimundo's arms, which was not a bad thing, because when he held me, he danced as if the tango wasn't about him holding me or me sometimes being pressed against him. Tango wasn't about him or me at all, really, it was about life. The beauty and the sadness of it. The sadness somehow making life even more beautiful, and the tango more beautiful than any music, so beautiful I thought maybe someday I would marry a man who danced tango, but not Raimundo, because he was too old.

17

Me and Saint Sam in the Dark

All the time we were dancing, Uncle sat in his chair staring at his unlaced shoes and looking resentful. After the last song ended, Raimundo gave me a little kiss on the cheek, like a kiss from a breeze, and said I was becoming a very good dancer; but Uncle frowned and turned the tape player off without even asking us, and got my blankets out of the old black suitcase. I'd done more than enough dancing, he said, and it was time for me to go to bed.

The mats were thick and brand-new, with a clean fresh reedy smell and no bedbugs, but I wasn't used to sleeping up high. When I rolled over, they scrunched down to one side or the other, so I felt as if I was falling off.

I watched the candle burning in front of Saint Sam. Its flame wavered and leaped inside its glass, making Saint Sam's bony finger glitter orange in the dark. It pointed straight at me.

I wanted to blow the candle out, but I didn't dare. Besides it wouldn't have been right, anyhow, in Raimundo's house where he was being good to me.

In the front room, Uncle and Raimundo toasted to friendship. I didn't pay any attention to what else they said until I heard Raimundo say my name.

Raimundo said I seemed like a quiet girl, and Uncle said yes, I was quiet and, more than that, I could stay absolutely still for hours, which was difficult for a child. Raimundo asked if I was reliable, and Uncle said I was. Raimundo asked if I was smart, and Uncle said I wasn't. That didn't hurt so much to hear because Doña Celestina had said the opposite. But my own opinion was Uncle had it right. I had been smart when I was little, when I lived with my parents, but I wasn't anymore.

Raimundo asked if I was honest. Uncle said I was, and Raimundo said, "With everybody?" Uncle said yes, and Raimundo sighed and said that was too bad.

He asked if I believed the things Uncle told me, and Uncle said, "Of course; she believes anything I say," and Raimundo said that was good and a solution to everything.

They started talking about old times in the army then,

their voices rising, then sinking, getting louder as they drank more. At first I couldn't understand what they were talking about, even when I knew the words.

"We had to show the ears!" Raimundo said loudly, then lowered his voice. "You do your work, then you have to carry rotting ears around in the heat for days."

Uncle said, "I remember La Hortensia . . ." And kept talking very low. The only words I could make out were La Hortensia, La Hortensia, La Hortensia, which came up over and over again.

La Hortensia. The farm where Doña Celestina's husband had died.

But maybe there was another La Hortensia, someplace else, and it wasn't a farm and probably even if it was, Uncle hadn't been there, he was just talking about it. But I got scared, scared he'd done something terrible when he was young that he wouldn't want me to know about, and I pulled my blanket up over my face, in case Uncle came in, because I was afraid of what he would do if he found out I wasn't sleeping.

I moved just a little and the mats made a sound like dry corn shifting in a sack, but I was lucky. Uncle didn't come in, so probably he never heard it. I stuck my fingers in my ears so I couldn't hear him or Raimundo anymore. And then I tried to forget.

18

Nice Things

I only wanted to think about nice things. For instance, about Raimundo's bathroom, where I was.

It had a lock on the door. That was nice.

The soap was nice, too. Not round, waxy orange laundry soap, the kind Uncle and I used for everything, which would roll around damp afterward in his suitcase and come out the next day a little sandy, looking like a lost pumpkin. No.

Special soap, a big pink bar that smelled like roses. And next to it in a plastic bottle was something else nice—a special golden soap for hair called shampoo. I'd seen that sold in markets, but I'd never had any.

The water came out of the shower head, not really hot, it's true, but warm, as if sun had been shining on it. I used lots of pink soap and the rain from the shower washed it off. The golden shampoo smelled like apple blossoms and turned white and soft and foamy in my hair.

There was a towel just for me, that smelled clean, like sunshine.

There was a big mirror, full-length. I'd never seen a big mirror like that before. I'd never seen my whole self clear before—just my face sometimes, looking in the side mirrors of trucks.

In Raimundo's mirror I could see my whole body. There was a hollow spot at the base of my neck, where I used to think the demon was. I never knew that.

My arms and legs were long and thin. My hair wasn't frizzy—not the way it got from laundry soap. It fell straight, like dark rain, almost to my waist.

I stared at myself. My eyes stared back from the mirror with a proud look I never knew was in them.

I tried to make my eyes look humble, really humble, because I thought that was the way Raimundo and Uncle would like me. But I couldn't make the proud look disappear. Yet I never felt proud. Where was the look coming from? It seemed there was another person inside me, a self I didn't know looking out from my eyes. I liked her, but she frightened me.

I got dressed. When I went out to the front room, a woman who had to be Raimundo's sister was setting a basket down. She was wearing a beautiful red huipil embroidered with silky purple cats touching soft paws and fierce tails.

"Here's Rosa," Raimundo said. "Rosa, Dolores."

"A pleasure," we both said, as she picked up the empty rum bottles and shoved them behind the door.

She reminded me of a cat herself, cool and not eager to be friends.

Most women I'd seen did things with small movements, squeezing themselves little so they didn't take up much room, as if they wanted to show the men that they wouldn't be any trouble or get in anybody's way.

Dolores, on the contrary, soaked up a lot of space. When she unloaded her basket, Uncle and even Raimundo stepped back to make sure they weren't in her way.

She set out hot tortillas wrapped in a cloth, a plate with mashed black beans made into a velvety loaf, and a pan of chilaquiles—scrambled eggs mixed with fried tortillas and bits of hot jalapeño peppers. I brought plates and silverware from the cupboard. Uncle, Raimundo, and I sat down to breakfast.

Uncle tried the chilaquiles and told her they were stupendous.

She thanked him in her cool way and stood watching us eat. Watching me especially. It made me nervous.

"Are you comfortable here, Rosa?" she asked.

I was in a house with a roof and almost my own room, and a real bathroom. Most everything was very good. I didn't dare say I wasn't comfortable. Really, I was comfortable.

"She's fine here," Uncle said before I could answer. "She's in paradise."

"She has her privacy, too," Raimundo said. "Her own room."

"Shared with your saint?"

Raimundo said. "Rosa doesn't mind. Do you, Rosa?"

"I don't mind."

"An altar to money, that's what you've got," Dolores observed.

Raimundo jabbed at his eggs. "Money is freedom."

"To you," Dolores said. "To me, work is freedom."

"La loca!" Uncle muttered, and scrambled eggs dribbled out of his mouth, she'd surprised him so much. Then he apologized for calling her crazy, said it had just burst out of him.

Dolores shrugged. "No problem." She picked up her serving dishes from dinner the night before and put them in her basket. She turned toward me, swinging her basket in her hand.

"Rosa, thank you for washing the dishes. —Maybe tonight you could come to my house and help me carry the dinner?"

"She can't," Raimundo said, reaching for a tortilla. "She'll be occupied."

"How?" Dolores asked.

Raimundo dropped the tortilla, leaned toward Dolores. "Our business is your business? You're my caretaker?"

"You think I'd take that job on?"

Raimundo scowled. Dolores laughed. She rolled up the gold cloth she used to cushion her basket, formed it into a coil, and set it on her head. She rested her basket on top of the coil.

"Adiós," she said. "Don't buy out all the liquor in the town."

She walked down the steps, her basket not even swaying.

Raimundo stared after her, his owl eyes narrowing, and made a gesture of someone slitting a throat.

"Didn't I tell you, Baltasar? Long nose, long tongue! How she makes me suffer!"

After breakfast I did all the work I could think of to thank Raimundo for giving me a place to stay. I cleaned up the house. I even swept the walk.

Uncle and Raimundo sat on the steps watching me.

"Very neat and tidy!" Raimundo said. "A very helpful young lady."

"It's nothing," I said.

"Now you can go play."

I hated it that Raimundo said that, as if I were a child. Besides, even when I was little, Uncle never told me to go play. I didn't know how.

Uncle said, "You go—we have things to talk about."

I stood staring at them, holding the broom. I didn't want to leave, but I couldn't tell them no.

Raimundo reached into his pocket. "Your sandals are way too tight, aren't they? Go get yourself some shoes. And come back at four, not sooner."

He handed me sixty quetzales just as if it was nothing to him.

"Buy them loose or you'll grow out of them in a week," Uncle advised.

"Yes, Uncle. —Thank you, Raimundo, for the money."

Raimundo grinned. "You'll earn it."

19

Onions

In the market I bought a pair of shiny black shoes with big plastic pearl buttons over the toes. I put them on and threw my old sandals in a trash bin. I stood tall. I felt elegant enough to walk on rainbows.

People must have thought I looked rich. In the crowded aisles of the market, sellers were calling out to me, "Bananas, my darling?" "Sausages, my princess?" They talked that fancy to me in the San Sebastián market, and they couldn't even see my feet.

And then I fell off the rainbow. One minute the way they talked felt nice, and the next minute it made me anxious, and I wanted to run from them, run from all the attention as fast as I could in my brand-new shiny shoes.

I wasn't used to having things, and suddenly I had a lot—soap, hot showers, shoes, food, a house to live in.

I had been poor a long time, just as if I'd been created on purpose to be that way. Now God or Mundo or some other spirit was going to notice my shoes. That spirit would go on to notice that I was living in a house and had enough to eat, and it would tell me, "This wasn't our plan for you," and swoop down to carry away everything. Leave me even worse off than I was before.

"Pretty princess, come here! My little queen, do you want celery?"

I looked to the mountains that rose behind the market and saw a narrow path going up. I ran for it.

Dust settled on my new shoes and on the hem of my corte. Families passed me going down the mountain, barefoot or in sandals with pieces of old rubber from car tires for the soles. They carried heavy loads on their heads—things to sell in the San Sebastián market. They said buenos días, but they didn't call me darling or queen or anything like that. They didn't look at my feet.

I went on higher. My new shoes hurt, and I took them off and wrapped them in my shawl. I came to a big rock, where I sat down, my heart beating fast.

It was very quiet there. All the harsh noise of San Sebastián—the pickups honking, the vendors shouting—floated up lightly like a tinkling of small bells.

I could see the whole town all the way to the lake, and just outside it, the town of the dead—the cemetery with its tombs like little houses, blue and yellow, pink and red and green.

Now I'll know how to get around this town, I thought, in case Uncle goes blind again and wants me to lead him.

That thought seemed good, almost nice, until without my wanting it to, my mind started repeating "La Hortensia, La Hortensia," as if it were the thumping of my heart.

To stop it, I walked. Barefoot to the lake through a street crowded with tourists and people selling them all kind of things. On past docks where local people and foreigners were getting on and off big white boats. Up a shady road with orange trees on either side. To the edge of town and a yellow bridge across a narrow river.

Suddenly, all I could smell was onions, delicious, like a thousand of them frying. Alongside the bridge in a field, a family—a mother, a father, a girl, a little boy, and a baby—was harvesting onions, washing them in the creek and then tying them in bunches with strings made from izote leaves.

I asked if I could help.

"We can't pay," the father said.

I told him I didn't care about pay, I just wanted to help.

He looked surprised, but said it was all right.

I sat down by his daughter, who told me her name was Elena. She showed me how to put the bunches together, and how to tear the tough izote leaves into strips, discarding the edges that could cut our hands.

It was cozy, being with them, all of us sitting with heaps of onions around us, the green stems fanned out like feathers; the baby boy nursing at his mother's breast when he wanted to or covering his eyes in onion stems and peeping out at everyone.

When lunchtime came, the family shared their food with me. They lifted fear off me. I stayed with them until I knew I had to go.

20

The Game

I put my new shoes on just before I got to the door.

Uncle and Raimundo looked up when I came in. I lifted my corte a few inches above my ankles so they would see my shoes, but they didn't pay any attention. I had to say "Look at my new shoes!" to get Uncle to look, and Raimundo didn't even bother. He leaned close to me, wrinkling his nose.

"Son of a turtle, what is that stink?"

"Green onions," I said.

"What did you do, *roll* in them?"

"I helped a family bunch them," I said. "I just wanted to help them, that's all."

Raimundo took hold of my hands. "Green hands!"

"A little bit."

He dropped my hands. "Messed up just when there's work to do! Change your clothes and wash!"

"Okay," I said. I started toward the bathroom.

"Where are you going?"

"To wash," I said.

"The sweet soap in there's not strong enough for your condition," he said. "Use the laundry soap and wash in the pila."

"Careful!" Uncle warned. "There's a vicious animal out back."

"The dog's not vicious, Baltasar," Raimundo said. "It just reacted to how you treated it. But don't you go touching it, Rosa! Being doggy will be no improvement on your smell!"

I was ready to burst out crying from the way he talked to me. I turned away so he couldn't see my face, and out back, I leaned against the side of the house and cried.

The dog was tied to a rope, and it started jumping and barking like mad.

I figured Raimundo would blame me for the racket it was making. I told it to hush. It stopped barking and whined.

It was a girl dog—a big brown collie with a cream-colored chest, her hair long and brushed to a shine. She had a blue leather collar and a piece of a cut leash dangling from it.

I took water from the pila in a bowl and put it where she could reach it. She stuck her nose into the water and lapped it up. Water dripped from her nose. She didn't look fierce; she looked grateful.

I washed at the pila till the skin on my hands was sore, and then went in and changed my clothes. But Raimundo said the onion smell wasn't gone yet. He told me to go ask Dolores for some parsley from her garden, but not to talk to her.

She lived on the same street, a few houses down. I went to her gate and knocked.

"Buenas tardes. Raimundo wants some parsley," I said.

I hoped that wasn't too much talking. I didn't see how I could ask her for parsley and not speak.

We went into her back garden, and she picked a few sprigs and asked me what I'd been doing.

Nothing, I told her.

"Nothing?" she repeated. "You're in this big new town and you've done nothing! Well, what are you going to do?"

"Nothing," I said.

She looked at me, trying to figure out if I was rude or just stupid.

"I'm not supposed to talk to you," I said.

"Why?"

"I don't know, I'm just not supposed to."

"Who said?"

"Raimundo."

She sighed. "I'll talk to *you*, then."

She hadn't given me the parsley yet. How could I say no?

"But if you repeat what I tell you, I'll deny I ever said it—so don't you blab it, understand?"

I nodded.

"Rosa—watch out for my brother! He's smart and handsome, and he can be charming—but the only person he loves in this whole world is himself."

I wished she hadn't said it. Maybe it wasn't true, anyhow. Once my hands didn't smell bad, which was my own fault, he would be nice again.

She put the parsley in my hand and walked me to the gate. "Be careful, Rosa, that's all I can say. Don't do anything you don't want to do. And some things you might want to do—don't do those, either."

I didn't know what she meant. She must have seen that in my face.

"I mean, if you think of getting close to Raimundo, don't. Because even if you try your best, you won't be able to. He won't let you."

I took the parsley to Raimundo. I thought maybe he wanted to smell it so he wouldn't smell onions anymore, but it wasn't that. He handed me a cup with sugar in it and told me to wash my hands again with water, sugar, and the parsley, which would take the onion smell off me.

All the time I was rewashing, the dog whined, and I felt sorry for her. I felt sorry for me, too.

In the house, Raimundo and Uncle were still sitting around the table. They both sniffed at me and said I was finally all right, and Raimundo gave me some lotion to rub on my hands. It had hardly any smell at all, but it felt good.

"Now your hands match your new shoes," Raimundo said, "nice and shiny, all ready for work!"

Was he being nice? Was he being not nice? I couldn't tell.

"You need to practice for the first job," Uncle said. "It's like a game."

It sounded like fun. Nobody ever played games with me.

"Ready?" Raimundo stood up. He pulled a thin little booklet with a blue plastic cover out of his back pocket, whirled it in front of my face, and then stuffed it back into his pocket.

He covered his eyes with his hands and challenged me to get it out of his pocket fast, without his knowing.

It didn't look so hard. I held my hand very flat and just overlapped my forefinger and my middle finger. I thought I got it out clean, but Raimundo said he felt it.

So I did it again.

Uncle started coaching me, telling me to stand close to Raimundo, very close, almost under his arm, and touch his shoulder with my other hand sometimes to distract him.

Raimundo said I was getting better, but he guessed he'd become too sensitive to my movements, and I should try taking the booklet out of Uncle's pocket.

Uncle wore loose pants, not jeans like Raimundo. I got

the little booklet out of Uncle's pocket the first time and he didn't feel a thing. He said I was very good.

Raimundo said we partners should sit down and talk. He poured Cokes for all of us and said I was a fine intelligent young lady with a lot of talent. Just the night before, that would have thrilled me, but now it didn't.

He opened up the little booklet so I could see it.

"Now, this little booklet, you know what it is?"

"No," I said.

"Well, all the foreigners who come here have a little book like this."

"Do they?" I said. Really I didn't care.

"Yes."

"They're supposed to carry it with them all the time," Uncle said. "It's called a passport. It gives them permission to visit different countries and go back again to their own country."

"You know what a country is, don't you?" Raimundo asked.

I told him I did. "There's a lot more than one in the world," I said. "Guatemala is a country, the United States is a country, and so is Mexico and maybe—California?"

I didn't like him anymore, but I couldn't keep myself from trying to show off so he would like me.

"Could be," Raimundo said. He took a sip of his Coke.

"The old foreigners that come from the boats in the mornings, they've come a long way. They come in big ships on the Pacific Ocean to the Guatemalan coast, and then on buses to the lake, and then on small boats to San Sebastián. By law, they have to carry their passports with them. Usually in a pocket. A pants pocket or sometimes a jacket pocket. You can see a little bulge where they keep it."

He put on his fancy black jacket, and stuck the passport into all his different pockets so I could get to recognize the outline of it.

He looked at me sorrowfully with his round owl eyes.

"Now, Rosa, as you must know by now, the world is unfair. Fortunate people have passports, but a lot of other people who would like to have passports can't get them. They can't go see the world at all."

"A pity," I said. Really, I couldn't manage to care about the unlucky people who couldn't go see the world. For sure I wasn't going to see it either.

Uncle said, "If a foreigner loses his passport here in San Sebastián, that's no problem to him, because he can get a new one practically for free."

"Where from?" I asked.

Raimundo sighed. "From the government of his country."

He bent the passport and made the pages flip by like cards being shuffled. I took a big drink of Coke from my glass. I thought of the collie tied up and how she was probably thirsty again.

"But that old passport that the person lost—pay attention, Rosa! Quit gulping your drink!—has a value. Another person will pay a lot of money to have it. So helping one person lose his passport and helping another person have it is a way to make money and do good."

Raimundo smiled at me.

"Let her see it," Uncle said.

Raimundo handed me the passport we'd been practicing with. It had a picture inside it, a color photo of a face. Not Raimundo's face.

"The person that buys a passport from us will be one who looks a lot like that," Uncle explained. "That's why he can use it."

"Women's passports are good, too—worth getting, and sometimes they're in purses, easy to get—but the price is better for men's," Raimundo said.

"Why?" I said.

"Because men get in more trouble," Uncle said.

Raimundo didn't like that answer. He gave Uncle a scowl.

"Because men travel more," he said.

"Say you just reach into a pocket and get one man's passport, you'll be helping another man become a traveler," Uncle said. "And if you get five passports from five men, that might be enough work for a year. You wouldn't need to do it again for a long, long time."

"It would be s-s-stealing," I said. I could feel the heaviness that Doña Celestina had cured me of, coiling in my throat.

When I was little, my mother told me you don't touch

other people's things without permission. You don't take them unless they give them to you. Sometimes in my life because of hunger, I'd taken an ear of corn from a field or an avocado from under a tree. But I never stole from anybody's pocket. I never took anything from an old person or a child, or anyone. Never.

Raimundo sighed. "You have talent, Rosa, and besides that, small fingers. Your uncle and I, we've grown too much."

"I could do it if I ask permission," I said.

Uncle grinned. "I give you permission."

"I-I-I would have to ask permission of the person who had the passport. H-h-he might be kind. He might want to help somebody else have a passport, who knows? S-s-so that person could travel, too."

Uncle's and Raimundo's faces lost their smiles.

"I told you she isn't bright," Uncle said.

"You never know," I said, "someone might give me permission."

"You can't ask the owner for permission, Rosa," Raimundo said. "That's not part of the game."

"You have to just take one, quickly," Uncle explained. "Just the way you were practicing."

"The three of us are partners, Rosa," Raimundo said. "A team."

"You've always been a good girl," Uncle said. "You've always obeyed me."

"One for all and all for one," Raimundo said.

I couldn't talk; I just shook my head.

"*A mi manera o a la carretera,*" Raimundo rhymed. My way or the highway.

"*Pagamos, mandamos,*" Uncle added. We pay, you do what we say.

I shook my head. Tears welled up in my eyes.

Raimundo swirled the Coke in his glass. "I hear you've never been to school, Rosa. If you live here you can go. Work in the morning, go to school in the afternoon. No problem."

"The old sheep from the ships are slow," Uncle said. "Not observant. Like the old lady in the market in Nebaj, remember? They'll be halfway across the Pacific before they ever miss their passports. On their way to China, or Japan, or California."

"You can do it, Rosa!" Raimundo said. "What do you say?"

I couldn't say anything. I couldn't even shake my head anymore, and I was sure the demon Doña Celestina took away was back in my throat.

Raimundo shrugged and looked at his watch—a big fancy watch with a band that looked as if it was made out of links of gold, but who knows if it was real.

"Don't worry, Rosa," he said. "We'll work this out. Right now it's time to go to church. That's why you had to wash so much. A person going to church shouldn't smell like onions, don't you know?"

21

Lucky Mouse

A wool bag with the image of a lion and the words
"San Sebastián" crocheted into it hung from Raimundo's
shoulder. It bulged with a heavy weight.

I wondered what was in it.

We passed Dolores, watering flowers in her front yard.
I would have waved, except Uncle and Raimundo each
held me by a hand.

Dolores waved, though, and Raimundo waved back.

He swung my arm up and down in a friendly way.

"Dolores talks too much," he said softly. "Don't you be
like that. Bad things can happen to you if you're like
that."

What he said scared me, but it made me angry, too.

We kept walking.

"Where is the dog from?" I asked Raimundo.

"We bought it in the market," Raimundo said.

"I never saw anybody sell a fancy dog like that in a market."

"So? There're lots of things you've never seen," Raimundo said.

"What are you going to do with her?"

"Sell her," Uncle said.

No matter what Raimundo claimed, nobody sells a dog like that in a market.

We got to the church plaza and sat down on a stone bench under a palm tree. Between Uncle and Raimundo, I felt like the thin middle of a sandwich.

The church was a lot bigger than the one in Nebaj, with carved stone figures of saints high up in the outside walls.

We weren't far from the entrance. There was a street to our left. A block away it ended at a cross street with a tiny park and a long building right behind it.

I could have run the block from where we were sitting, to the park, in a minute.

Uncle looked all around. I never heard him ask so many questions as he did that night.

" 'Mundo, what's that tall building right behind us?" he asked.

"That's the old bell tower," Raimundo said. "The bell broke in an earthquake and they never fixed it and they blocked the entrance off."

"What's that building on the right?" Uncle asked.

He meant the building across the church plaza from where we sat. It was a big new brick building attached to the old church.

"It's the priest's house," Raimundo said.

Uncle grimaced. "He lives so close to the church!"

"All that padre cares about is jogging," Raimundo said. "He goes to bed at ten o'clock every night and sleeps like a rock."

Uncle stared up the street to the park. "What is that building behind the park?" he asked.

"The city hall and the police station."

"This church is very badly situated!" Uncle said.

"The police play cards all night," Raimundo said. "They wouldn't move even for an earthquake."

"If you say so." Uncle sounded doubtful.

"Rosa, have you ever been inside a church?" Raimundo asked.

"No, never," I said. "At least, not that I remember."

Raimundo said it was too bad that my first time I was going to have to stay for hours, but when you have a job to do for your partners, you do it.

"Right?" His owl eyes stared into mine.

"Right." I said it, but it didn't seem right. A partner should have a say. I wasn't a partner. I was just a girl they were bossing.

"Raimundo tells me there's a very valuable statue in the church that has termites in the wood," Uncle said.

"Yes," Raimundo said. "Holy María of the Lilies is going to ruin. I've spoken to the good padre about it many times, but he just won't listen."

The good padre. The good father. Maybe he really was good. Like my own father had been.

"The only way to save it," Uncle said, "is to take it out secretly and get it fixed."

"And bring it back?" I asked.

"Of course," Raimundo said. He smiled into my eyes.

He told me the whole plan, how he and Uncle were going to rescue the statue, and how I was going to help—hiding in the church till after it had closed, and then going out and leaving the big entrance doors unlocked for them. If a guard found me in the church after it closed, that would be no problem. All I had to do was say I'd fallen asleep praying.

"In that case," Uncle said, "come back to the house right away and tell us. If you don't come by midnight, we'll know it's safe to rescue the statue."

They made it sound easy.

"There are things for you in Raimundo's bag," Uncle said.

Raimundo held it open. I saw a hammer, a pair of pliers, a screwdriver, a saw. A flashlight and a knife. A watch, not fancy like Raimundo's. The watch was so I'd know the time to leave the church.

Raimundo explained to me how to use the pliers and

the screwdriver. I might need them and the hammer for opening the door of the church, he said, if I couldn't do it just with my bare hands. When I left the church, I should leave the bag and all the tools behind.

Raimundo reached into his jeans pocket and got out an extra key to his gate and gave it to me. It was a sign of how much he trusted me, he said.

Uncle said I'd always been trustworthy and obedient.

"That's the best way to be," Raimundo said.

"When you go back to the house, your supper will be out on the table waiting for you," he added. "But we won't be there because we'll have already left to rescue the statue. We'll come back in the morning."

I didn't like the idea of being alone. Alone in the house, alone for hours in the church.

They must have seen the fear in my face. Raimundo patted my shoulder and said I was a good girl to help rescue the statue.

Uncle said, "Don't worry. At any hour, the streets are safe here."

Raimundo grinned. "There are no criminals at all in San Sebastián, thanks be to God."

The church was long and narrow, with small stained glass windows just below the ceiling. We went into an empty pew near the back and knelt.

At the front, there were two big vases of flowers on the

altar and tall white candles burning in silver holders. A boy in black-and-white robes reached between the flowers with a tall candle snuffer and put out the flames one by one.

Above the altar was a statue of Jesus nailed on a cross, with blood drops and rays of gold coming out from around a crown of thorns on his head. Raimundo whispered low to Uncle so the people scattered around us praying wouldn't hear. The statue of Jesus was well done, he said, but it was new and had no value.

We walked around the side aisle of the church, which had a row of other statues high up on the wall. We got to a beautiful one of a woman holding a bouquet of white lilies, and wearing a blue cloak edged in silver.

"That's Holy María of the Lilies," Raimundo whispered. "She's four hundred years old at least. The work of a master carver from Spain."

Uncle nodded as if he knew about such things. "A treasure," he murmured, "a real one, don't you see, Rosa?"

We moved on quickly, not giving that statue any more attention than the others.

Near the front of the church, we came to a small wooden room with a roof—like a little house right inside the big house of the church. Raimundo whispered to me it was the confessional. Outside he had already explained what it was for—how after they'd done wrong, the Catholics went to a kneeling bench at an outside window to confess their sins and ask forgiveness. The priest who forgave them in the Christian god's name sat inside the little house.

Raimundo delicately touched the latch to its door. It was unlocked, the way he'd said it would be. When the church was empty, I was supposed to hide in there.

We returned to the church entrance and looked at the two flat iron crosses riveted to the thick planks of the door panels, the heavy iron bolts that were pulled shut every night to close the doors. "Fine work," Raimundo whispered. "Colonial."

Uncle looking at the bare surrounding walls, spoke so close to Raimundo's ear that I could hardly hear him.

"No wires. No electricity. No alarm."

Uncle and Raimundo knelt on the stone floor and made little goodbye bows to Jesus on the cross. Raimundo handed me his heavy bag.

"Pray for your mother's health, Rosa," Uncle whispered loudly, going out the door. "We'll be at the hospital."

I wished he hadn't said anything about my mother. To make me think about how I hadn't seen her for years, and she might even be in a hospital.

I went to a pew near the confessional and sat with my hands folded and my eyes half-closed. A guard walked around, his footsteps echoing.

After an hour, everybody had gone out but me—even the guard.

I walked quickly to the confessional, opened its little door, and hid.

In the dark I could feel a chair, and on the chair, a cushion. I sat down. Sat down where the priest was supposed to sit.

The confessional had one window covered in cloth. Some air came in through that, but not much. The tiny room smelled of incense and mustiness and patience and sweat. Stale old sins floated around in the darkness.

It was hard to breathe. I sat without moving, without making a sound.

Footsteps on the stone floor echoed against the stone walls.

"Everyone out! Closing! Closing!"

If the guard had been paying attention, he'd know I hadn't left.

He'd open the door to the confessional very soon. Then I'd have to pretend that I'd fallen asleep in a place where I wasn't supposed to be.

I heard the clicking of his shoes on the tiles, coming closer, getting softer. He had passed by. There was a thud as the big entrance doors closed and the bolts were pulled shut.

Raimundo had told me the guard would go out the side exit. I heard the sound of that smaller door closing, being locked with a key.

I was alone.

I groped in Raimundo's bag for the flashlight and shone it on the watch. 11:10.

I was supposed to stay hidden in the confessional till midnight, but I couldn't stand to do it. I opened the confessional door and went out.

Small candles flickered in little red glass cups in a metal rack at the front of the church. That was the only light.

I heard a chittering sound and switched the flashlight on. A tiny mouse, caught in its beam, ran down the aisle and disappeared behind the altar.

He must have had a home back there.

I went as close as I could to Holy María of the Lilies. I shone the flashlight on the merciful lines of her mouth—and then on her strange blue eyes, the bouquet of lilies in her belt, the delicate white hands with long fingers that she held out to me.

She seemed to be alive. All statues have life in them, that's what a lot of people believe.

But Raimundo and Uncle said she was full of termites.

I looked for signs of termites. If a statue or any piece of wood has them, you can tell. First there are little holes the termites drill into the wood. Later, after years, whole pieces of wood get eaten, paint and all.

Holy María of the Lilies was perfect—her lips, her eyes, her hands, the bouquet of lilies, and the blue of her robe. The paint looked old and had fine cracks in it, but there weren't any holes. None.

I looked into her eyes. I spoke to her.

"Holy María, do you have termites? They say you do."

She didn't answer, except to look through the flashlight beam, with her merciful, mild face.

"They say they're taking you to get repaired so you can come back here where you belong."

She looked at me wisely, but said nothing.

"They're taking you, so don't get scared. They don't want you to get damaged. You'll stay perfect and— But I don't think they're taking you to get repaired.

"They say you're very valuable. Maybe they're going to sell you to someone with a lot of money. Probably you'll be in a nice place, even if you won't be with the people here who love you, even if nobody will pray to you or talk to you.

"They say they're going to take you in a pickup. They're going to wrap you in a heavy blanket so you don't get hurt.

"You and the blanket will be covered in corn, so nobody will see you. I think you'll go far away, maybe travel on a ship to another country—even if you don't have a passport. You'll never be here again."

When I lowered the flashlight, shadows moved like tears along her face.

"I have to do it, Holy María, they told me I have to."

She looked as if she didn't understand. Maybe, being in the same place for four hundred years, she couldn't. I tried to explain to her.

"I won't have a place to live if I don't do it. They won't keep me."

She looked sad about that.

"Probably you thought you were safe, being here four hundred years. What will happen to you, it's not so bad, really it's like what happened to me. The police will look for you, but they'll never find you. Nobody here will ever see you again."

Did she care about being stolen? I couldn't tell. She didn't make a sound.

I started to wish anyone, anything, even the little mouse, would move and come to me.

Probably the mouse was like me, scared.

Still, he was lucky. Lucky to live in a church his whole life and not know human ways or have to guess them. Lucky not to be scared a person would hit him or leave him. And maybe he wasn't really scared of anything, just ran because he liked to run, his blood warm and cozy in his tiny heart.

How lucky to be him.

I shone the flashlight all around. Shadows moved, shadows of the saints on their pedestals, stretching all the way to the ceiling, beckoning.

I didn't know what they wanted from me.

I shut my eyes in front of Holy María of the Lilies and begged her to give me some sign, to make a miracle.

And suddenly she did. My eyes were still closed, but I

could see and touch her smile, all soft and changing, and see her skin, darker, and her hair changing till it was black and wound in ribbons like Doña Celestina's, and instead of a gold crown over her blue veil she had a red shawl like Doña Celestina's.

I asked Holy María for a greater miracle, for her to talk to me, and she did.

She said, "Tzunún Chumil, I'm Doña Celestina and I'm Holy María of the Lilies and I'm your mother, too; and you know, Tzunún, what you must do."

The bolts of the huge doors slid right open.

Small as a mouse, free as a mouse, I looked up at the moon and the stars.

22

In the Moonlight

The priest was a young, sharp-faced man in a sweatshirt and jogging pants.

He wasn't like my father at all.

He frowned at me. "Why are you bothering me, coming to the rectory at this hour?"

"It's about the statue," I said, "the statue of Holy María of the Lilies."

"What about it?" he said.

"I want to know if she has termites."

He got very angry. "Is this a joke?" he said. "Who told you to come here and knock on my door?"

"Just tell me if a man ever told you she has termites."

"The statue is perfect. Nobody ever told me anything about termites. Now go away, and if you must, come back in the morning."

"I'll go away, but first I have to tell you—at one o'clock, and that's not long from now, two men are coming to take away the statue. Because she has termites, that's what they say.

"And I can't stand out here, they mustn't see me!"

The priest pulled me inside his house and closed the door.

"The bag with their tools is in the church," I said. "That's how you can know that it's true."

"And how do you know about all this?" he asked.

I told him.

When I had explained, he said he was grateful. He guessed I must be tired and hungry, too. He took me into his kitchen and got me some cookies and a glass of tomato juice, and then he sat me down in his living room, in a big soft chair with leather cushions.

He said in a minute he would have to make a phone call.

"To the police?" I asked.

No, he said, he didn't have much confidence in the police, they were lazy and sometimes corrupt. He wasn't calling them, he was calling the sacristan.

"What's a sacristan?" I asked.

"He's the caretaker of the church," the priest said. "He's the bell ringer."

"He wouldn't hurt Uncle and Raimundo, would he?" I asked.

The priest hesitated. "Not him. No."

"Uncle and Raimundo, maybe they really only want to rescue the statue. That's what they say."

The priest smiled at that. "Don't be naïve, child," he said. "You know better. You know better, or you wouldn't have come to me."

"I don't want them to be hurt!"

I looked at the glass of tomato juice on the table by the couch.

"Would you please take the glass away?" I said. "I can't drink it."

He moved it onto another table, but I couldn't stop looking at it. It seemed as if things were moving in it. Bloody things. Ears.

"What's the matter, child?" the priest said. "What are you thinking about?"

"I don't want them to know I told! I don't want them to know ever!"

"They won't learn it tonight," the priest said, "but soon they will. I'm sorry about that, but they're bad men, anyhow—you need to stay away from them."

I forced my eyes away from the tomato juice.

"If they find out I told, they might kill me," I said.

"How could they kill you? They're going to be in jail," the priest said.

"The police might jail me, as well," I said.

"That won't happen. You're a child, a victim."

That's what he thought. The police would say I was a partner.

He asked me if I was a Catholic. I said no.

He said anyway I was a very good human being to have warned him. Even if I wasn't a Catholic. I'd done a very courageous thing. And he knew that because of coming to him, I'd lost my home. But he could find me a good place to live, and maybe I could become Catholic, but only if I wanted. And I didn't have to worry about the police. If the police came into it, he would speak for me and tell them I had stopped a crime, not committed one.

He told me to wait for him while he went to his office and phoned the sacristan.

I ate all the cookies, trying not to look at the tomato juice.

The room had a TV and books and newspapers and a footstool with an old weaving across it. On the wall there was a cross with a figure of Jesus on it, with big holes that nails had made through his hands and his feet. He had his ears, though. Nobody had taken his ears.

What if the priest was wrong, and the police arrested me? If they locked me in the same cell with Uncle and Raimundo, I'd be dead in the morning.

The priest was leaning forward in his chair, his body all angles, his mouth close to the phone. He saw me leaving and waved at me to stop, but I ran as fast as I could, out of his house and across the plaza, looking everywhere for a place to hide. And then I saw one.

I broke a rotten board that blocked the entrance. I squeezed into the old bell tower and climbed the dusty stairs to the tower room and looked out from its arch. I saw the church, and straight down the street the little park, the city hall, and the police station. The streetlights and the moon lit the plaza and the street with a pale dusty light.

A cold wind blew through the bell tower. I shivered and pulled my shawl tight around me. I'd left Raimundo's watch in the church. I wished I had it. Along the street by the side of the church, a small white cat ducked into dark bushes. A night hunter.

A pickup with no lights turned onto the street and parked alongside the church. The driver got out carrying something dark. I could tell by his walk it was Raimundo. The passenger got out. I knew him by the way he moved, too—Uncle. He took something from the back of the pickup—a ladder. Raimundo helped him carry it.

They went into the church with the ladder and pulled the big doors shut. Everything was quiet then. The white cat came out of the bushes and dashed across the street.

My warning must have gone for nothing. The priest hadn't believed it, or the sacristan had talked him out of believing it. Nobody was going to save Holy María of the Lilies.

In the shadows where I saw nobody, someone coughed. I raised myself up on the stone window ledge and looked directly down. There were men right below the bell tower, maybe twenty of them, some with machetes. One of them turned and looked up, stared right at me, it seemed. I froze. He yawned and lowered his head. I stepped farther back from the arch.

In the distance along the side of the church, other men were moving quietly to the bushes that the cat had run from. They stopped there, where no one looking out the front doors of the church could see them. They were about thirty feet from the pickup, no farther.

One of the big church doors opened a crack. A man stuck his head out, peering all around. It had to be Uncle. He didn't walk out in the open to check the side of the church where the men were hidden. He just opened the door wider and beckoned to Raimundo, and they came out quickly carrying a long, heavy bundle. They lifted it into the pickup bed and shoved it into the pale stuff that gleamed back there. They dug their hands into the pale stuff and spread it around.

The men alongside the bushes and the ones below the tower ran toward them. One caught Uncle by the neck. Raimundo must have heard them coming: he opened the door of the pickup and jumped in. Somebody grabbed the door, but it didn't open.

Men swarmed around on all sides. The pickup started with a roar, and the men in front of it jumped clear. Raimundo was going to get away for sure, I thought— but while the motor raced faster and faster, the truck never moved. Men behind it had picked it up and were holding the back wheels off the ground. Just as if it were a toy, and Raimundo a toy driver.

Somebody broke in the front window with a rock, and dragged Raimundo out. Two men held his arms. Somebody shone a flashlight in his eyes. Behind the pickup, Uncle was lying on the ground. Somebody must have hurt him, and I'd never meant for him to get hurt. I only wanted to save the statue.

Suddenly the church bell pealed, so loud I jumped and covered my ears, and I could see high up in the church, straight across from me, a square opening and the shadowy shape of the bell ringer, his whole body swinging as he rang the bell.

Hundreds of people were running to the plaza from all directions, men and women both, shouting "Robbery! Thieves!"

The priest came down the steps from his house.

People shoved in close around the pickup and the group holding Uncle and Raimundo. Around the outside of the crowd stood the men with machetes. I couldn't see Uncle or Raimundo anymore, but I heard groans.

"Who are they?" someone yelled.

At first there was no answer, just a lot of angry muttering.

"Raimundo Rosales and an unknown!" a woman shouted.

"Raimundo Rosales!" lots of people yelled, and other voices shouted things I couldn't hear.

"Raimundo Rosales! Burn him!" someone yelled. "Get gasoline!"

I heard the priest. "No, my good people, no!"

But people were arriving with lit torches, and it looked as if some were leaving, going for gasoline. A space opened around Uncle and Raimundo, and I could see them again, lying on the ground in the middle of a circle of orange light.

I never meant for them to get hurt, neither one of them.

Everybody in the crowd was silent, waiting for the burning.

"There's another thief somewhere," someone shouted. "There was another, hiding in the church!"

I was the one. If they found me, would I burn?

"No, my people, no!" shouted the priest. "There were only two!"

They must have believed him. Nobody looked for me.

Two women ran up with big white plastic bottles—the gasoline, I guessed—and the crowd parted and let them through. Men pulled Uncle and Raimundo to their feet and held them while the stuff in the bottles was poured all over them. Bad as they were, I didn't want them to burn, and tears came to my eyes. I asked Holy María herself to save them, and just then the bell in the church rang out so loud I thought my ears would burst, and a siren whined ominously into the night, and arcs of blue and red light glanced off the church and the buildings across the street.

A police car drove slowly from the park, inching its way through the crowd, with police on foot beside it. People backed away from them. Maybe they had guns. And one must have had a microphone, because I heard his voice booming.

"Citizens of San Sebastián! You must turn over your prisoners! If you burn them, it's murder! We'll arrest you all. Go home!" He repeated that over and over.

The police car forced the crowd to move until only the men holding Uncle and Raimundo were in front of it. The police took Uncle and Raimundo and shoved them into the car. The driver didn't bother to turn it around, he just backed it down the street to the park.

People ran alongside the car shouting. I couldn't hear what they said.

I couldn't see when Uncle and Raimundo were taken through the park to the station, but I knew when it was done. The crowd roared a sad roar. People stood in the park and the street, with more still arriving.

"Give them to us! Give them to us! Give them to us!" the crowd chanted.

A policeman climbed onto the station house roof with a microphone. He promised that justice would be done and begged the crowd, as law-abiding people, to go home.

In some towns crowds don't go home. Sometimes they set fire to police stations and roast everyone inside till the police let *them* make justice.

The people of San Sebastián were merciful, though. They stopped chanting. Slowly, they left the park.

Men carried the statue of Holy María of the Lilies into the church, many women walking beside them. Police went in and came out carrying the ladder and something else—maybe Raimundo's bag of tools. The young priest shook everyone's hands, and the sacristan locked the church doors.

The street emptied; the plaza was silent. The white cat came out from under the bench by the palm tree and sat with her ears pricked, licking her paws.

23

So Long, Saint Sam

Raimundo's house was dark. I used the key he'd given me and opened the gate. I listened for a sound, any sound from inside, but there was none. I opened the door.

There was a small lamp by the beds. I set it on the floor and lit it. It almost blinded me, it was so bright. I threw a sheet over it to hide the light from anybody passing.

On the table there were a whole lot of bones on a platter, and two pork chops still not eaten. Also three small potatoes and a couple of tortillas. I found a plastic bag in the cupboard and loaded the food into it.

In the back room, Saint Sam's candle was still burning. I gathered all my belongings and rolled them into my blankets. I found a cord in the cupboard to tie the bundle and set it and the food by the front door so I could leave fast.

I didn't want to stay there another minute, but I had to find the little piece of paper that Uncle owed me.

I went through the old black suitcase, which was under his bed in the front room. Wherever that paper was, or if it was, it wasn't in that suitcase.

Maybe he'd given it to Raimundo. I moved the lamp and searched Raimundo's things, too. Everything in the cupboard, everything in the bathroom, everything Raimundo had under his other bed. Black boot polish and a polishing rag. An old pair of cowboy boots. I reached inside the left boot and touched paper. I pulled the paper out. A hundred quetzales. It wasn't mine, so I didn't take it. I shoved it back into the boot and turned out the light.

I heard someone breathing and the sound terrified me. Then I realized the someone was me.

I went back into the room I'd shared with Saint Sam, lifting up the mats I'd slept on, lifting up the white cloth on Raimundo's altar table.

Nowhere in that house was there any little paper that was mine.

In the light of the black candle, Saint Sam pointed his bony finger at me. Telling me I was no good. Telling me I would always fail. I'd had enough of him. I blew his candle out.

I heard something. Not breathing. More like the absence of breathing. There was somebody near me. I knew it. I ran for the bedroom door and collided with a body.

A whimper came out of me—as if I were a toy somebody had squeezed.

"Hush!" It was Dolores.

I couldn't get by her.

"Don't tell Raimundo!" I begged. "Don't tell him I blew the candle out!"

"What are you doing here? You've torn up the place! What are you taking from here?"

"Nothing. —Just the food," I said. "Don't tell him I blew the candle out!"

Dolores sighed. "I won't tell him. —But why have you torn the place apart?"

"Uncle has a paper that belongs to me. I was looking for it. But I didn't find it."

"I'm looking for Raimundo's money," Dolores said. "To get him a lawyer."

"There's some in one of his cowboy boots under his bed," I said. "A hundred quetzales."

I thought she'd say I must have taken some of his money, and then search me and take my very own hundred away from me, but she didn't.

"He's in deep trouble this time," she said. "And so will you be if you stay here."

She wasn't going to keep me from leaving. I didn't need to fear her.

We walked into the front room.

"What are you going to do?" I said.

Dolores shrugged. "Help him. He's my brother."

"Please don't tell him you found me here."

"I won't," Dolores said. "And don't tell me where you're going because I don't want to know."

I picked up my bundle and the bag of food by the door. "I've got the rest of the food," I said. "It's your food."

"You keep it," Dolores said.

The collie started barking out back.

"Uncle said that dog is vicious."

"He must have mistreated her. I fed her tonight. She's a nice dog. We'll go give her a little pork now to quiet her down. And then you take her with you."

I was still a little scared of the dog.

"If she stays with you, she'll be a protection," Dolores said. "Anyhow, this place is no good, not even for a dog."

The collie quieted when I fed her half a pork chop. I untied her, and she licked my hands.

Dolores helped me put my bundle on my head. The three of us walked to the gate.

"I hope you'll be all right," Dolores said. "I wish you well."

The dog and I went out the gate and up the lane.

24

Where Nobody Goes

We kept to the back streets. We got to the yellow bridge and crossed that, then started down to the lake. The dog trotted at my side, her ears pricked to sounds in the night.

Some small animal slithered through bushes, and she dashed after it, disappearing in the tall grass along the river. She didn't come back.

I stood in the road waiting for her. I called to her loudly; I didn't care who heard.

"Come, dog! Come!"

She didn't come. I couldn't wait for her. But it was so hard going down the road alone.

I thought I'd never see her again—but when I got near the lake, there she was, a flash of white and brown in the moonlight, running to me. I dropped everything to hug her. I begged her to stay with me. I told her I was giving her a name. I called her J'aal—"Beautiful" in my language, Kaqchikel.

When we got to the safe place it must have been about three in the morning. The moonlight was shining on the little bright-colored tombs that looked so much like houses, and the pale white crosses that rose above them.

The gate was closed, but J'aal and I crawled under.

We passed by many tombs, with shadowy bouquets of flowers in tin cans and glass jars set in front of them. I found an open space and spread my blankets out, one under me, one on top. I reached into my bag of food and took out the pork chop and a potato and ate them. I gave J'aal a potato.

There was nobody but us in the cemetery, but I could feel something moving. I sensed something, then heard something.

At night, souls go wandering, that's what some people say. The souls in pain, the ones the Christian god doesn't care for but the Christian devil doesn't want either, they wake up at midnight and their graves open, and the ghost of the pallbearers they had at their funeral carry them around once more in coffins lined with velvet and pearls.

And suddenly I saw one sit up in his coffin. Soon he'd say, "For pity of a penitent, take my place!" And if I listened with pity in my heart, I'd jump into a coffin and take his place. He'd run away clapping his rotten hands, disappearing like smoke in the wind.

But it seemed as if J'aal hadn't heard anything, hadn't seen anything.

Maybe it was just stories. Maybe it wasn't even true.

Anyhow, they say the souls in pain won't tempt you if you aren't afraid.

I lay down flat between the graves with J'aal next to me. But I couldn't sleep—she was too far away. I begged her to lie down on top of me, and she did. I wrapped my hands in her fur. Her body warmed me. It made me feel safe, the way I felt when I was little, when I'd slept between my parents.

I was so glad to be with her. She was heavy, but so warm.

25

Toy Dogs

We finished all the food in the morning, sitting under a willow by the lakeshore.

Far out on the water a fisherman paddled a canoe, stopping every now and then to check his nets. He and the canoe were just black shapes against the sunrise.

Everything was at peace.

But not me. I'd woken up crazy.

I wanted to see Uncle. I wanted to make sure he was all right. When I remembered him the way he really was, I knew better. But I kept remembering him the way he really wasn't, and I wanted to see him so much that almost nothing else mattered.

Once when I was still little, in I don't remember which town, I was outside a school where I saw a piece of magic that scared me. A man was sitting on a stool with a flat piece of cardboard across his knees. On the cardboard there was a bar of some grayish metal about as long as my hand, and on the farthest corner from the bar there were three tiny toy dogs about as big as my thumb.

Kids crowded around the man to see the toy dogs.

The man told us that the grayish metal bar was the lord of the dogs and could command them and make them fly. If you didn't believe it, you could bet with him for just ten centavos and maybe win your money back and a toy dog, too—besides the ones on the cardboard, he had many others that he took out of his pants pocket and showed us.

A lot of kids did bet, and he put all their ten centavos in another pocket.

The man put his face close to the bar and whistled to it, a spooky sound like the wind. I guessed he was trying to wake up its power. But he didn't succeed—the bar just sat, and the toy dogs just sat, too. The little kids thought they were going to win. Myself, I thought the man was going to move the cardboard by bumping his knees and make the dogs slide, but he didn't move his knees at all, he just moved the metal bar in a circle with his hand. Slowly he inched it a little closer to the dogs, and a little closer—and snap—all of a sudden the three toy dogs flew across the cardboard and stuck to the bar.

The man swooped the bar into the air, and the dogs didn't fall off. He whirled the bar around his head, and the dogs still didn't fall off. They just stuck, no matter what. He held his arm high above his head and pulled the dogs away from the bar just a little bit and let go of them—snap! They flew back to the bar on their own. Flew right through the air. It was some kind of witchcraft. But it was true what he said—the bar was the lord of the dogs, and all the kids who'd bet lost their money.

I was afraid that for me Uncle was magic like that bar. If I got too close to him, I'd fly to him, straight through the air. If I got near him, I'd stick to him and do what he said, no matter what.

I didn't want to stick to him. I wanted to go to Doña Celestina.

But if he got out of jail, Nebaj was the first place he'd look for me. He'd ask about a girl that might have a collie dog, a girl wearing Kaqchikel clothes.

I imagined him coming into Doña Celestina's house, telling me, "Come on, Rosa! Time to go!"

What would I do?

Nebaj was the one place where I'd never be safe.

"J'aal," I asked, "what should I do?"

She looked at me, puzzled. I put my hands into her fur and petted her. I put my face against her neck, and it seemed as if I learned the answer from her.

There's more to life than being safe. There's being happy.

26

Marcos

On the road to the yellow bridge, kids went by us, carrying bowls of wet corn to the mill for tortillas. Men went by, on their way to their fields with heavy hoes over their shoulders and machetes in their hands. Women went by, carrying enormous baskets of fresh flowers on their heads to sell in the San Sebastián market.

J'aal and I reached the bridge. A big truck was parked by the side of the road, full of onions.

Elena's father was talking to a heavyset bearish man with thick black hair.

I stood there with J'aal till Elena's father noticed me.

"Buenos días, you don't look good," was the first thing he said.

"I'm all right," I told him.

"And now where are you bound?"

"Back to Nebaj," I said.

"I thought you were staying here," he said.

"It didn't work out."

"Why?"

"On account of a problem with my uncle."

Elena's father's soft round face looked softened even more from his concern. "Maybe you can talk to your uncle. Maybe the problem can be fixed."

"It will never be fixed."

"Are you afraid he's going to punish you for something?"

"Yes. No. I have to leave."

"And what will you do in Nebaj?" he said.

"I have a friend there."

Elena's father looked doubtful.

"Brother, she knows what she wants," the heavyset man said. "I had to run away myself when I was her age. I'd be dead if I hadn't."

"Maybe you can help her, then," said Elena's father. "She's a good girl, Marcos."

"I'm going to the capital," Marcos said. "I can take you part of the way."

"And my dog?"

"No problem."

I told him we'd go with him, and thanks for the ride, Don Marcos.

"I don't like titles. Just call me Marcos."

"Thank you for the ride, Marcos."

"It's nothing." He put my bundle in back with the onions and helped me and J'aal into the cab of the truck.

Elena's father wished me well.

Marcos started the truck. In a minute we were in San Sebastián.

I looked out the window, so tired that my eyes kept blinking shut. Between blinks I had a vision of a girl, and the girl was me. She was standing somewhere in my future, beckoning for me to come to her.

"It'll be a long trip for you, but I hope a good one," Marcos said.

"I hope."

Marcos slowed for a speed bump, his truck heaving itself up and over. We passed the church. I pressed against J'aal's fur, hiding my face. I was scared the priest would see me and shout to Marcos to stop the truck.

"Big excitement here last night," Marcos rumbled. "I was here, I saw it. Two thieves tried to steal a statue from the church, and half the town turned out to capture them."

"And the police, too." I tried to make it sound like a question, but I didn't succeed. Marcos didn't seem to notice.

"Finally," Marcos said. "Any time they think they might get shot, they're very slow to turn up—not that I blame them. A lot of times the thieves have better weapons than the cops."

He honked once and swerved the truck around a man

with a cart selling watermelon and mango slices, then stopped.

"Which do you want, watermelon or mango?"

"Mango," I said. "Please."

The man with the cart passed mango and watermelon slices in the window of Marcos's truck, and we drove on.

"Before the police came," Marcos continued, "the people were going to burn the thieves. The same criminals rob and steal and murder and escape jail over and over. It gets to where the good people can't bear it—working and working just to be robbed and have their loved ones killed. There's no justice."

"Were they hurt?"

"No," Marcos said. "Fortunately not. They beat the guys up, but nobody got a scratch."

"I mean the robbers," I said. "Did they get hurt?"

"Those thieves? Not bad enough to need a hospital, is what I hear."

We were almost out of town now, passing the big Conquistador Hotel and the gas station.

"At the market this morning, everybody was talking about it," Marcos said. "Some people said a girl gave a tip about the robbery and then disappeared."

I stared into J'aal's fur.

"Everybody wants to find the girl—to thank her. The mayor wants to give her a medal."

I looked up at that, I couldn't help it, imagining a whole lot of people shaking my hand and somebody as important as the mayor of San Sebastián pinning a medal on me.

Marcos glanced at me again. "But sometimes for somebody who gives a tip about a crime, a medal isn't worth it," he said. "Sometimes it's just wiser to leave town."

"Yes," I said. "It's wiser. It would be. For that girl."

The truck stalled. Marcos did something to a tube sticking out of the floor. That changed the sound of the motor, and the truck charged up the mountain like a goat.

Marcos asked me if I was Catholic, and I told him no.

"Protestant?" he asked.

I said I wasn't that either.

"So you worship Mundo?" he asked.

I said I didn't know.

Marcos said, "My religion is think, do good, and use your brain."

A big boulder nearly as wide as his truck had fallen into the road from the mountain above. Marcos drove around it carefully and speeded up again.

"Help your neighbor, too, if he's not a skunk."

It didn't sound like a religion. "That's all?"

"That's it. And you know why I came to it? Because of the war. So many people around where I lived made sacrifices to Mundo and the ancestors. When the war came, they got massacred. What did the ancestors do for them? Nothing.

"A whole lot loved Jesus, and prayed and gave donations and went to church all the time. Some of my neighbors went into a church to escape the army and the guerilla fighters, and they got massacred in there, every one. What did Jesus do for them? Nothing."

"Maybe he did. Maybe he did in the next world," I said.

"Maybe he did," Marcos said, "but my religion is, don't wait for anybody else to take care of you. Think and use your brain.

"I left home myself when I was twelve," he said. "I started out with nothing, but I used my brain, and now I've got my own truck."

I couldn't picture myself ever having a truck. And no matter how he'd survived just by using his brain, I wanted help in the world besides me.

"It's a hard life you've got," Marcos said. "I know that."

I nodded and blinked back some tears.

"You'll be all right, though," he said. "I can tell."

"How do you know?" I said.

"With some people I sense it. They have kind of a shine to them. A shine from inside. You have it."

"I never saw any shine to me," I said.

"The person who has it doesn't know," he said. "But you have it. It's there."

27

The Lesson

We passed through two little towns, and then we got to the crossroads where we had to go different ways. Marcos parked at the side of the highway.

I didn't know how to open the door of his truck, because I'd never ridden inside one before. He had to come around and let me and J'aal out.

He gave me a bottle of pure water to drink on the journey and pointed off into a cornfield at a pila where some country women were washing. "Your dog needs water, too," he said. "Maybe those women will give you some."

He got my bundle out of the back and set it by the side of the road.

The odor of onions swirled up from it.

"My bundle stinks of onions," I said.

"That's not a stink, that's a good smell!" Marcos said. "Never did anybody any harm."

It was time to pay him. I pulled on the string around my neck for my little purse. I held out the only money I had left, the beautiful clean hundred-quetzal bill that Doña Celestina had returned to me.

"How much do I owe you?"

His eyebrows went up in surprise. Then his thick hand dove down like a hawk and plucked the hundred right out from between my fingers.

"This will be fine, muchas gracias."

He'd taken all my money! I couldn't get to Nebaj without it! How could he charge so much for a short ride that he had to make anyway? I had thought he was nice—but he was just like Uncle!

"You're more than welcome!" I said bitterly, and then I spat, spat right on the ground, the way men do. I hoped the ancestors or Mundo or somebody would know I was reverse-talking and make Marcos pay for what he'd done.

J'aal raised her head, her ears pricked up. She knew that something was wrong, she just didn't know what.

Marcos waved the bill in front of my stony face, making a tiny breeze with it.

He looked so smug and gleeful I wanted to punch him right in his big jelly roll of a belly where it flabbed out over his belt. But if you're a kid you don't ever hit a grownup. You don't dare.

"You didn't want to give me your hundred?" Marcos asked sweetly, just as if he didn't know.

I shook my head.

"So then why did you?"

"I didn't give it to you, Marcos! You took it!"

"Not true," Marcos said. "You could have held on to it when I reached for it, but you didn't. Why not?"

I shrugged.

"Don't shrug, tell me!"

"You gave me a ride, you wanted the money, you're the grownup."

"But that's not a good reason," Marcos said. "Is it? Not a right reason to hand over so much money for a short ride?"

I told him no, it wasn't right for me to give it to him, and it wasn't right for him to take it, either, so why did he?

He put the hundred away in a little compartment in his belt. "To teach you a lesson. So you'll learn to use your brain and hold on to what's yours."

He got a thick wad of crumpled bills out of his back pocket and counted them out in ones and fives and tens. He handed them to me.

"How much do they come to?" he asked.

"A hundred," I said.

"Are you sure?" he said. "That's a lot of bills and I counted them fast. Count them again!"

I counted them. They came to a hundred. I held the whole wad of bills out to him.

Some older boys walked by, glancing at us from under their hats.

"You got back something that was yours that you thought you lost," Marcos said. "Why are you standing there holding all that money out where someone can grab it?"

"I don't know what you want me to do," I said.

"I want the money back," Marcos said.

It was a nightmare beginning all over again, and I was so tired, I just wanted it to be over. I started to give him the wad of small bills, but he pushed my hand away.

"Maybe I want it back, but so what? What do *you* want? That's what matters!"

In my life, what I wanted almost never mattered, and usually, beyond remembering my parents and wanting to be with them, I didn't even want.

This time, though, I knew what I wanted. I curled the small bills into a tight roll and put them into my little purse.

"Good for you!" Marcos said. "You didn't wait to ask for permission to take what was already yours! You didn't wait for Mundo or the ancestors or Jesus to give it to you! You got your head in gear! You got your wheels moving!"

A bus pulled up, the helper leaning out and shouting the names of the towns where it was going. A small crowd surged toward the bus, a couple of men jumping out of the back of pickups to take the bus instead.

"Do you know how to travel?" Marcos asked.

"I don't know. I think so, but maybe I don't."

"Well," Marcos said, "let me tell you. First off, you should know you can't take a bus. If you had a chicken or a small pig in a bag, it would be different, it could go up on top, but the dog is too big, she can't ride up there."

"I don't like buses, anyhow," I said.

"So you need to go in pickups," Marcos continued. "Well, don't get into any pickup where you're the only passenger. Get into one that has a few people, so you know you're not going to be tricked and carried off to who-knows-where to do who-knows-what and ruin your life forever."

I nodded. I never thought of that before. I just went where Uncle said, and if there was paying to do, he paid. When I had been with him, I didn't have to think. Maybe I did think by accident sometimes, but I didn't have to.

"And don't get into the worst-looking pickup you see, because the brakes may fail and then where'll you be— down at the bottom of a ravine with your neck broken, maybe!

"Find out the price before you take the ride—but don't pay till the ride is over. If there aren't any witnesses, a crooked driver will just keep the money and not even give you a ride. If you let a crooked driver take a big bill like the one you let me have, unless you have witnesses you'll never get anything back, no matter how much you scream and holler and spit on the ground."

He knew I'd been disrespecting him and reverse-talking, but he hadn't hit me for it or anything.

"So you just show one little bill at a time, only what you really need at the moment, and that way you won't get cheated. See what the other people are paying first before you pay."

"They'll charge extra for J'aal," I said, "because she's big."

"Right," Marcos said, "they'll try, but you say she can lie down around your feet, and she only takes up half the space of a person."

We went over to the better-looking pickup at the crossroads—one with wooden benches along two sides of the truck bed. Two women with babies on their backs were already sitting on one bench, and the driver was talking to them.

"You watch and remember so you can do what I do," Marcos said.

He talked to the driver and found out he was going on the road to Nebaj. The driver wanted to charge full human price for J'aal, but Marcos told him nobody ever charged full human price for a dog, and that J'aal could fit under the bench.

"Full price for the dog," the driver said.

"Let's go check on the other pickup," Marcos said to

me. But before we could even leave, the driver of the pickup with benches sighed and said all right, he'd charge just half price for J'aal.

"Agreed," Marcos said. "You're not leaving right away? The girl needs to go get some water for her dog."

The driver said he'd wait for me.

Marcos walked me back to the side of the road. "Take care of yourself," he said. "Think of what you want. Defend yourself in this world." He spoke softly, close to my ear. "Remember—you've got a shine to you."

He looked at his watch and said he had to leave. I started running across the fields with J'aal, to get her water.

He was gone when I got back.

That's when I figured it out.

He was a good man. He wasn't like Uncle. Not at all.

28

My Road

Just the way Marcos had told me, I kept all my money in the purse around my neck, and handed out only what I needed to spend. Nobody stole from me, but it still took almost all my little bills. J'aal and I didn't eat anything the whole day, because I was afraid we'd run out of money if I bought food.

At dusk we got to the big town of Santa Cruz del Quiché. The only pickup going on to Nebaj looked new, but when night fell, it turned out to have no lights at all. A man in the front seat held a flashlight out the window so the driver could see the road.

In the back we were swallowed by darkness, except when a car passed or a house was lit along the side of the road. Air rushed against us, very cold, and colder yet when it started raining, big drops of water splatting out of the sky. The grownups got out sheets of plastic and covered themselves and their kids as best they could. I didn't have any plastic myself. I'd left mine behind at Raimundo's. I huddled against J'aal in the rain until a woman reached out and pulled her family's plastic sheet over me.

When we got into Nebaj, it was really late. I slid out of the truck, shivering in the rain. J'aal jumped out and shook herself, scattering raindrops. Everybody who'd traveled with us said "buenas noches" and ran toward their houses. After that, there was nobody on the streets.

The moon was so buried under clouds that I could hardly find the lane to Doña Celestina's house. My legs were stiff and weak. By the time I got to Doña Celestina's gate, my head felt strange, too, as if it were dissolving and about to float away.

There wasn't any light showing in the house. I was afraid of waking Doña Celestina, but I pulled the bell rope anyway, pulled it hard. The sound of it shocked my ears.

Doña Celestina opened a little shutter in her front door and peered out.

"It's me, Tzunún!" I called.

She ran down the walk toward me, barefoot and in her nightgown, a candle in her hand. I was hanging on to the gate, trembling from tiredness and the cold.

"Are you all right? What's happened?" she said.

"Excuse me for waking you, Doña Celestina, I had to.

Uncle's in jail in San Sebastián—so I had to leave there. I don't have a divided heart anymore, at least I think I don't. Please, will you let me stay with you?"

She took the padlock off the gate, her face looming very near in the light of the candle and then receding in shadows.

"Tzunún," she said kindly, but I didn't understand the rest. Danger, concern, I don't know what-all words she used, it was just one big jumble to me, and I didn't know if she meant for me to come on in or keep walking.

She motioned me through the gate, and I knew that meant come in, but when I let go of the gatepost I felt myself falling, falling to the bottom of the night.

I heard the voice first, cheerful and full of energy, with a swinging rhythm to it, like someone rocking a baby.

"Tea of fox weed right away, Celestina, that's what I would say, to stop a cough and open up her sinuses. Lemon juice, honey, and garlic together to break the fever. And at night a tea of mallow leaves or linden flowers to calm her."

"Soup, that's what I've fixed—vegetables and greens with lots of garlic."

"Good. She needs to eat, but nothing heavy."

Somebody was sick, and Doña Celestina and the other woman must be taking care of that person. But I wished they hadn't bothered me about it. I'd been in a vast space made of roses, where celestial beings of perfect goodness had cared for me, and I'd had no body and no needs.

My hands touched the edges of a narrow bed. I pulled at the blankets. I was hot, so hot, but once I got the covers off, I started shivering.

Doña Celestina covered me again.

The other woman touched my forehead with a fine and gentle hand.

"It's nice to see that you're awake! —I'm Amalia."

She had a wide, kind face. Brilliant ribbons with pompoms on the end were wound into her gray hair.

I tried to answer her, but Doña Celestina hushed me. "Not now, Tzunún—rest your throat."

"There's always a weak point," Doña Amalia said; "each body has one. Hers is the throat."

Maybe it was true. My throat felt big, and it was hard to swallow.

I looked around. The walls of the room were made of boards, with cracks between them where light came in, and more light coming in at the door and at a small window. Where was I? I wished I knew.

Doña Celestina must have seen me wondering.

"You're in my house, in the room that was my daughter's—behind the kitchen. Your dog is outside, on the patio. In a minute I'll let her in so she can see you."

I smiled.

"You slept all night and almost the whole day, Tzunún. It will soon be night again."

She lit a candle and set it on the table by my bed. "—There's no electricity in this room.

"Doña Amalia's gone to make a special tea for you. She's a midwife, and she cures with plants."

"Gracías." My throat felt like a rough blanket. Only one word and my voice was almost gone.

Doña Celestina sat down on the end of the bed. "Tzunún, you don't need to talk," she said, "just nod to answer me. All right?"

I nodded.

"When you got here last night, you asked if you could stay with me. Remember that?"

I nodded.

"Do you still want to stay with me?"

I nodded again, looking into her eyes.

"I know you're not well yet, but I need to tell you now, so you won't worry or be scared. —Yes, you can stay with me!"

I nodded.

"You'll need to help me and be honest with me. I think it will work and be good for both of us—and if not, well, we'll have tried and there'll be no blame on either side. All right?"

It might not work, that's what she was saying. But also, she was saying it could work, she was giving me a chance.

I nodded.

"Good," Celestina said. "It will take a while, but we'll learn each other's ways, I think."

She went to get J'aal, who licked my hand and sat with me.

Doña Amalia brought in the tea, and some extra pillows that she put behind my back. Doña Celestina came with the soup. I ate and drank and then once more I slept till morning.

29

The Search

Out at the patio table, with J'aal at our feet, we talked.

I told Doña Celestina and Doña Amalia what had happened in San Sebastián. They said Uncle and Raimundo would be sentenced to long prison terms for their crime. I asked if the court would want to put me in prison, too, and Doña Amalia said no, I was a child and not guilty of anything.

"The court in San Sebastián will want you—but only as a witness," Doña Celestina said.

My coffee cup shook in my hand. "Don't make me go back there! Please!" I was terrified of seeing Uncle and Raimundo again, of saying things against them in court while they listened, hating me and planning revenge.

Doña Celestina touched me, steadying my hand. "I won't make you go, Tzunún. Not if you don't want to. The court doesn't really need you. From what you say, there are dozens of other witnesses."

"The court doesn't know where you are," Doña Amalia said, "and we won't tell. Nobody can find you to make you a witness."

"In a way I'm glad that Baltasar's committed a crime," Doña Celestina said. "Now I don't have to worry that he can make trouble for me for keeping you."

She smiled.

"So I'll never have to see him again?"

Doña Celestina hesitated. "Last night I asked the seeds again about you and him. They still say you're to find him a treasure before the end of the year. So I have to think that somehow, he may get loose."

"The seeds aren't always right," Doña Amalia put in.

"Mostly they are," Doña Celestina said. "I don't want you to worry, Tzunún, but the most dangerous way to live is not knowing life's dangers."

I was scared, and the fear must have showed in my face.

"You just lead your life the way you need to lead it," Doña Amalia advised. "There's no use being afraid of whatever's hidden around the corner. Back in the war years, I got scared of going out at night to take care of my patients, but I went anyway. I decided I wouldn't meet Death hiding in my house like a nothing. If I had to meet

179

him, I'd meet him on my sacred road, doing the work God gave me."

"Tzunún," Doña Celestina said, "if you do see Baltasar, it doesn't mean you're going to die. If you ever do cross paths, try to get that little paper that he owes you. The seeds say he still has it."

I asked if she knew what the paper was about. She said she thought that the paper came from where I came from—the town where I was born. But she didn't know more than that.

Then Doña Amalia asked where I was born, and I said I didn't know, except that the first word in the name of the town was "San"—only I knew it wasn't San Sebastián.

Right then she and Doña Celestina started talking in Ixil. Doña Amalia left, and in a little while she came back with a thick telephone book. A neighbor had one.

Doña Celestina, who could read, opened it up and looked up the names of all the towns that began with "San." She read them off to me, slowly, telling me to say if one sounded familiar. I listened very carefully, but none did.

"Maybe you're trying too hard," Doña Celestina said. "Don't listen so carefully."

And I tried it again, but I didn't recognize a single name. And no people with my last name were listed in any of the towns.

Doña Amalia thought we should send letters to all the city halls of all the "San" towns anyway, asking about

Chumils and telling about me; and over the next few weeks we did.

Doña Celestina wrote the letters, and Doña Amalia paid for the stamps. It was a big effort that took a lot of time and almost fifteen quetzales. It was a good idea, too. But we never got any answers.

30

Nebaj Girl

Doña Celestina did her best to protect me from Uncle and
Raimundo.

She introduced me to her neighbors. She said I was her
godchild, and had come to live with her. She told them
threats had been made against me, and if anybody came
around asking for me, people should say that she, Doña
Celestina, lived alone, and that they'd never even heard of
me. The neighbors promised to help out, and to let us
know if anybody came asking questions.

I was afraid that if Uncle and Raimundo came looking
for me, they'd ask around town for a girl wearing blue
clothes, and people Doña Celestina didn't even know
might say they'd seen me. Doña Celestina dug deep in a
cedar chest she had in her bedroom and found a huipil

and a corte from Nebaj. She unfolded them, the fresh smell of cedar filling the room.

"My daughter wore these as a girl," Doña Celestina said. "I wove them myself."

The corte was deep red, with fine lines of yellow through it. The huipil was embroidered in green and red with many little triangles of silk.

I put them on.

"You look beautiful," Doña Celestina said. "Any stranger who sees you will think you're a Nebaj girl now."

I showed Doña Celestina the pieces of my hummingbird cup that had exploded in Santa Cruz and asked her if she thought what happened was a sign to me. She said yes, it was a sign and I'd understood it right—it was about my being divided and needing to be whole. While I glued the cup together, she said a prayer over it—a prayer for me to stay whole and safe.

Every few days I asked her exactly what the seeds and the ancestors were telling her about Uncle—if they still said I was going to find him a treasure before the end of the year.

She said that prediction hadn't changed. But the seeds didn't show Uncle coming to the house. Maybe, she said, there was some way I'd find him a treasure without even having to see him.

I felt better thinking that. Anyhow, Doña Celestina didn't leave me free time to worry.

She gave me jobs to do. She taught me to make black bean soup and how to cook rice and make salads. I swept and cleaned and washed our clothes. Sometimes I went to Doña Amalia's house when she needed me, and helped her prepare herbs she'd gathered, setting them out in the sun on her patio to dry, and then tying them in bunches and hanging them from the roof beams in a shed out back.

Every day Doña Celestina taught me more of the language of Nebaj, Ixil. Some days she had many people waiting to consult her, so I didn't see her until night. When she had money, sometimes she gave me a little so I could buy things for myself.

She wanted me to go to school. I couldn't attend public school without a birth certificate. But she had heard about a special school for child workers, where I could go without having to show any proof of who I was or when I was born. She took me there.

A few hours every day I studied at that school with a lot of other kids my age. The kids were all from Nebaj, but because they were poor, they worked. Part of the year, they were migrant workers—they went with their families down to the lowlands, the hot humid Pacific coast, to pick cotton or oranges or cut sugarcane on big plantations. Mostly it was because they were away so many months that they'd never gone to school.

Our teacher was a young man from a country that I'd never heard of, called Holland. He spoke Spanish and a little bit of Ixil. He taught us numbers, and the letters, and gave us each a special reading book that the government of Holland had made for us, in Spanish and Ixil. He said the people in Holland, way across the ocean, knew our government wasn't going to give us any reading book, and they were sorry about that and had asked their own government to help us.

He showed us on a big map where Holland was, and how far away it was from Guatemala. I thought it was amazing that people in a country I'd never even heard of knew about us and wanted to help us.

Doña Celestina said my school was a good school, and my teacher was a good man. She said she was working with a group of women to try to get a better government in Guatemala and more good schools, like the one I went to. I worried that the government and the army would get angry at her and the other women for that.

She said times had changed. The war years were over and it was safe to have ideas. "Besides," she said, "we're women and we don't have any guns. And anyhow, I'm like Amalia. If I meet death, I won't meet him hiding in my house, I'll meet him on my road."

In the evenings, by the light in the kitchen, Doña Celestina helped me read my new book from school. After that it would be time for sleep, and I'd go to my own room with a candle, and get in bed, and blow the candle out.

That was the bad part, when I got scared all over again. I'd listen to the leaves of the trees in the garden brushing against each other and think it was the sounds of Uncle and Raimundo, coming for me. Or I'd hear J'aal make a little moan out on the patio and think it was because Uncle and Raimundo were there, slitting her throat before they came into the house. Then I'd think they were inside my room, come to take me away, and Doña Celestina would never even know, she'd be sleeping.

I was ashamed, but finally I told Doña Celestina I was scared. She said J'aal could be in my room at night, and stay right on top of my bed. That helped.

I had another fear, too, that I didn't tell her for a long time. I was afraid to go to the market, because of the old lady with the bad eye. Uncle had cheated her, and I thought if she ever recognized me, that old lady would get me put in jail, right there in Nebaj, for passing bad money.

At first I'd go to the market to help Doña Celestina carry our food home, as long as I could stay away from that store. But pretty soon I got scared to go there at all, and I made up excuses not to.

Doña Celestina got suspicious and wanted to know why I wouldn't go to the market. I confessed how Uncle had given the old lady the counterfeit bill, and I didn't warn the lady.

Doña Celestina told me yes, I'd done wrong, and moreover my guilt and fear of the old lady were killing me, and she'd do a cleansing for me right away.

She sat me down on a chair in the kitchen and told me to hold my hands palms up and my feet off the floor.

I did, and then she brushed me with a bunch of long-stemmed, fragrant basil leaves to clean the fear out of me, brushing the basil over my hair first and then brushing me down my whole body, sending the fears out the palms of my hands and out of the soles of my feet, and praying over me.

I felt good when she finished—peaceful. But Doña Celestina said the fears would come back if I didn't go see the old lady and make amends. She asked me if I had any money, and I told her I had two quetzales that I was saving to buy an ice cream. Good, she said, I could give it to the old lady—right away, while I was cleansed.

We walked to the little store. The old lady quick-stepped to the counter. Her feet were as bad as ever, but she didn't have an eye patch anymore. She didn't recognize me, but I was still very scared.

"I can't talk," I whispered to Doña Celestina. "Please don't make me talk."

She nodded.

Doña Celestina ordered a Coke, which we shared with two straws, drinking it from the bottle. She asked the old woman's name, and then talked to her about whether the government would ever get the roads fixed, and when the rains would finally end. The old woman, whose name was Marta, said she hoped the rains would quit soon, because they made her bones ache. She paid me no attention at all.

We finished the Coke and Doña Celestina paid. She said, "Doña Marta, this is my godchild, Tzunún Chumil, a good girl. Until just recently she was forced to travel with a bad man who abused her and who stole. He gave you a counterfeit bill about a month ago; I don't know if you found out."

Doña Marta got a very angry look on her face. "I found out! I wish I hadn't! More than what I earned that day I lost to him!"

"Tzunún couldn't warn you when he gave it to you, because he would have punished her, but she wants you to know that she's sorry. And she has something for you."

I set my two quetzales on the counter.

"Tzunún wants you to forgive her. —Isn't that right, Tzunún?"

"Yes. Please." I felt like there was an elephant in my throat, but I got the words out.

The old lady squinted at me with her lips bunched up as if she'd tasted something sour.

"She would give you all your money back if she could," Doña Celestina said, "but she didn't take it and she doesn't have it. The man who did is in the jail in San Sebastián—with no money, of course."

The old lady sighed and waved a hand in front of her face as if she were brushing away a fly. She said she'd been very angry about the counterfeit bill, but that she understood I couldn't have stopped Uncle from giving it to her. She forgave me, she said, and she was glad I was loose from that man, and she hoped I'd make my godmother proud by being an honest girl.

31

Birth

One weekend Doña Celestina went to the town of Cotzal to see her daughter's family. They didn't have enough space for all of us, so J'aal and I stayed with Doña Amalia.

The first morning, Doña Amalia said she was going to teach me to make tortillas. She heated the griddle over the wood fire, and she told me to watch her make the first one. I tried to keep my eyes on her hands, but instead of watching her, my eyes kept darting away to the woodpile in the corner of her kitchen.

"So now you see!" Doña Amalia said, and handed me a little ball of dough and told me to pat it the way she'd done.

I held my palm out flat to pat the tortilla, and she kept waiting for me to pat it, but I didn't. Both my hands shook. The little ball of masa dough rolled off my palm onto the floor.

"What's wrong with you?" Doña Amalia said, and my whole body shook.

She sat me down and said I had to tell her what was the matter.

I told her about a time when I was seven, when Uncle had hired me out to make tortillas for a lady. I'd burned them, and the lady had hit me in the face with a stick of firewood for that. Afterward Uncle had told me he was sorry he'd gotten me that job, and he'd rubbed the cut on my face with a piece of lime to disinfect it—but still I'd wound up terrified of making tortillas.

Doña Amalia put her arms around me. "I don't expect you to make them perfect the first time," she said. "Nobody ever does. And don't you know Doña Celestina and I would never hit you?"

We got up, and she showed me again, treating the dough very gently—not slapping it at all, just shaping and patting it softly. Just the way adults should treat children, she said.

I copied her and I learned.

That night a man knocked on Doña Amalia's gate. He told Doña Amalia his wife was ready to give birth, and asked her to come quickly. Doña Amalia, J'aal, and I followed him to his house out in the country, and I carried Doña Amalia's suitcase with all the things she used when she received a new child into this world.

The house had two rooms, a big kitchen that also had beds in it, and one other bedroom. Doña Amalia went to the pregnant mother in the bedroom while the man and his two children and I stayed in the big room, waiting.

Doña Amalia came out after a while and asked me to go back to her house to get mint, which the woman needed to drink in a tea so the birth contractions would speed up. Doña Amalia told me to take J'aal with me. To light my way, she gave me the little flashlight that she always wore on a cord around her neck.

J'aal and I started out. I carried the little flashlight in my hand and lit it often, every time we came over a rise to a dark hollow in the road. The moon cast shadows of trees on the road that reminded me of the night J'aal and I'd run from Raimundo's house. When I looked at the trees, I thought I saw Raimundo and Uncle together in their shadows. Every time, the light from the flashlight proved that they weren't there, but still I felt pursued, Uncle and Raimundo pressing closer, closer.

They were in the San Sebastián jail or else already in some prison. They had to be.

I got to Doña Amalia's house and went into the shed with J'aal, shining the flashlight around, because I thought Uncle could be hiding in there, but he wasn't. I got a big bunch of dried mint, and then I sat down on an old wheelbarrow inside the shed and held on to J'aal and breathed in the fragrance of all the herbs hanging from the beams. I felt safe in the shed. I didn't want to leave it. It had no windows, and I saw some boards I could wedge under the door so nobody would be able to force it open.

I'd stay, I thought, and open up only for Doña Amalia when she came back. She'd understand why I didn't bring the mint: that I didn't have the courage.

Only I had it in my hands, the mint that was supposed to go to the woman in labor, and it seemed as if it was reproaching me, telling me it had a purpose, and I was blocking that purpose.

I remembered what Doña Amalia had said about how she'd never be a nothing person hiding in her house, how, no matter what, she'd walk her sacred road. I got up and left the shed with J'aal. Together we went back to the little house in the country. And somehow on the way back I didn't get as scared of Uncle and Raimundo, and didn't imagine so often that I saw them, and didn't think they were following me—maybe because it wasn't just the mint that had a purpose. I had a purpose, too.

The man let me into the house. Doña Amalia came out and told me how to prepare the mint tea, and I gave her back her flashlight. When the tea was ready, I went to the bedroom door and knocked, and handed the tea to Doña Amalia. I never looked at the pregnant woman, out of respect, because Doña Amalia had told me that giving birth is something just between the midwife and the mother, not for other people to see. Having other people around distracts the mother from the work of getting the baby to come out.

So I waited again with the husband and the children. We sat in that room, which was lit by just a kerosene lamp, for a couple of hours. The children fell asleep. The man had a radio that ran on batteries. He kept listening to a few different stations in Ixil and Spanish, all the time changing the stations as if nothing could suit him.

The pregnant woman screamed in the next room. The children woke up when they heard her screams, and the man turned the radio up loud so they wouldn't hear and tried to get them to play a game, clapping their hands.

Very soon the screams stopped, and the father and I knew that meant the baby had been born. A short while later Doña Amalia came to the door and called out to the husband that he and the children could come in, for just a minute or two.

I went in, as well. The mother was lying in the bed, holding the baby to her breast. It looked red and wrinkled and surprised. It had been swimming inside the mother for so many months and now it was beached on the shore of her body.

The little boy asked where the baby came from, and the mother said that an airplane had brought it. I could tell that his older sister didn't believe that, but she didn't say anything.

The father kissed his wife and the baby, and then we went out, and soon Doña Amalia came out, too, with her little suitcase, and she put on her shawl and we left.

The girl followed us out the door, and asked would her mother be all right, because she'd heard the screams, and they worried her. Doña Amalia told her that the baby had come out from inside her mother, not from an airplane, and it had hurt, but that now the pain was over, and the best thing the little girl could do was go to sleep, and then do everything her mother asked in the morning, to help make her comfortable, and respect her mother always, for the sacrifice it took to bring a new life into the world.

The sun came up as we started home. Doña Amalia said that made a perfect time to collect herbs—didn't they look beautiful? I carried her suitcase and she bent to pick this leaf and that, telling me their names and what they were for—plantain weed for infected wounds; artemisia to warm the stomach; milk thistle to cleanse the liver; chicken herb for stomachache; wild lettuce for anxiety and bad nerves; rue for heart attacks.

Often I'd seen those plants growing. Some of them I'd noticed around a spring on the way to Nebaj with Uncle. But I never knew their names or what they were good for till that morning.

A white-and-red butterfly with enormous wings landed on the front of Doña Amalia's huipil. It stayed there, poised over her heart, even as she nearly touched it with her hand.

"It's a sign," she said.

"Of what, Doña Amalia?"

"Red is the color of joy, and white is the color of peace," she said. "God's showing me he's happy with me!

He's telling me that I did good work last night. He's glad I'm still walking my right road."

When we got to her house, I could hardly stay awake, but she was full of energy.

Over breakfast I asked her if I could become a healer with herbs, like her. She said I could learn something about them, sure—but to actually do it, I'd have to have a gift and a dream: a dream to show me healing was my special gift; and later, other dreams that would teach me my own ways to use the herbs.

She asked me if I'd been frightened walking alone in the dark, and I said I had, a little bit.

"You were brave to bring the mint," she said. "I know you have worries sometimes."

She took her little flashlight off her neck and hung it around my own.

"This is for you," she said, "a special present to remember last night—and how you helped a mother give birth and didn't think only of yourself."

32

Ants

One afternoon at Doña Celestina's, I heard J'aal outside my room, barking. I ran to her and saw a huge brown spot on the floor—and the spot was moving.

It was ants, a river of them, an army of them marching through my room and under its plank wall to Doña Celestina's kitchen.

I stomped my foot near one, and it stood still. I knelt down next to it, as close as I could, and shone my flashlight on it. It was red-brown and big for an ant, with a slit-like mean mouth and two curved claws that stuck out between its jaws to grab things. It was horrible.

In an instant it was on the move again, crawling across the floor in that ugly groping, crooked way of ants. I ran to get the broom to sweep it and the whole lot of them outside, and called for Doña Celestina.

She came running from her consulting room. "Nasty creatures! They'll be in the kitchen and into the bean pot and the coffeepot and crawling through the tortillas, and we'll have no clean food and no peace!"

I swept harder. The broom knocked hundreds or maybe thousands of them back toward the door to the patio garden, but Doña Celestina said that was no use, the broom wouldn't stop them, they'd just keep coming.

In the kitchen she put wood on the fire and set two pots of water on to boil, while I swept ants away from her feet.

When the water boiled, she threw both pots across the brown swarm. Hundreds of ants fell on their sides, scalded, shriveling, and dying. The rest turned back.

"Excelente!" Doña Celestina exclaimed. "They'll tell the ones outside not to come in here. I don't know how they do it, but they talk to each other."

I swept dead ants and water out of the kitchen and out of my room, while Doña Celestina followed me around, wiping the floor with a mop, frowning and scrubbing hard.

I was learning to read her face. Something was bothering her.

"The ants—they're a bad sign, aren't they?" I said.

Doña Celestina pressed her lips together in what she meant to be a smile. "Maybe not. They like to come into houses in the rainy season."

"But the rainy season's almost over. I can see by your face that they're a sign of something, and it's not good."

"Let me worry," she said; "don't you worry."

"What are they a sign of? Tell me!" I said.

"Death," Doña Celestina said. "When they come into a house, it's a sign that somebody's going to die."

That night in my bed I had a dream of Uncle trying to get into Doña Celestina's house, shoving the door down. She and I pushed back as hard as we could, but the door was breaking, the hinges splitting right out of the wall. He was going to come in for sure. And then I woke up.

Even with J'aal by my feet, I didn't want to stay in my room anymore. I went into Doña Celestina's and woke her and told her my dream.

"It doesn't mean he's coming here," she said. "It's a warning, that's all." She got out of bed. "The seeds say he's not coming here, but who knows?"

In the kitchen she took the machete from the woodpile, and also a big spray can with drawings of spiders and roaches and ants on it. She said it was insecticide.

"It's too expensive to use on insects," she said, "but it's a fine weapon."

She showed me how I should use it if I had to—holding it head high, with a finger on the spray button, opening the door a crack, and spraying it directly into the eyes of any intruder. And then, while he was still blinded, I should open the door fully and use the machete. Split his head open. Just the way you'd split a log. Without hesitating.

I didn't want to go back to my room. I asked if I could sleep with her, and she said yes. And J'aal could stay there, too, she said. So we all slept together, and I felt safer.

In the morning Doña Celestina read the seeds for me.

I gathered them three times, and Doña Celestina arranged them on her table. I gathered them again, three more times, so she could be sure what she was reading.

I asked her what they said about Uncle.

"They say he's going to escape jail or prison, but they don't say when."

I bit my lip so I wouldn't say I was afraid.

"There's one good thing," Doña Celestina added. "The ancestors say he still has that little piece of paper that he owes you."

"Do they say I'll find him a treasure?"

"That's the strange thing," Doña Celestina said. "The seeds say yes, but the ancestors say no. I don't know what that means.

"The day 13 Q'anil comes up. The ancestors say I should do a special ceremony for you on that day, to protect you—a ceremony with prayers to Mundo and the Ahau."

"When?" It couldn't be too soon, that's what I thought.

"Next week. They say I should do it at the Two Rivers shrine."

I asked her why they said that.

"It's the place for the most serious problems."

Her tone scared me.

"Don't worry," she said. "The ancestors are looking out for you. They're already with you."

But for once her words didn't comfort me at all.

In the evening she said she thought my nerves were on edge. She made a tea of wild lettuce and told me to drink it all.

"I'm not the only one that needs it!" I said.

"If you think *I* need it, you're wrong!" Doña Celestina retorted. "I'm calm and I have no worries."

And then she took a cup and poured herself half.

33

Ceremony

After that we drank wild lettuce tea every night. I don't know if it helped Doña Celestina, but at least I didn't have any bad dreams.

I told Doña Amalia we were going to Two Rivers and asked what it was like. She said it was a beautiful place, out in the country not far from Nebaj. She hadn't seen it for a long time, she said, and she'd like to come with us.

The way she said it, though, was more as if she was *determined* to come with us.

"You don't want us to go alone!" I guessed.

"That isn't it at all," she protested. "I like excursions!"

If she had another reason for going with us, she wouldn't tell me what it was.

———

The morning of 13 Q'anil arrived, clear after a rainy night. With J'aal, the three of us set out. We were going to have a merienda, a picnic lunch, at Two Rivers. I carried food, and a ball for J'aal to retrieve. Doña Celestina carried things for the ceremony, and Doña Amalia had baskets for collecting mushrooms. She said that after the rain we should find lots of wild ones near the shrine.

The road curved beside sandy cliffs. A little way outside of Nebaj, it was almost completely blocked by a landslide, and we picked our way past some big rocks.

After that point, there weren't vehicles. I tossed the ball ahead of us down the empty road, and J'aal chased it. She was still a young dog, and she liked to play.

A rocky path met the road.

"We're almost there," Doña Celestina said. We turned off onto the path and walked up a hill. There were lots of trees around us. We got to a waterfall that leaped from rock to rock, leaving tiny drops of water hanging in the air like rainbows. Near it, in damp soil, Doña Amalia pointed out mushrooms—big flat orange ones the size of plates, and others, smaller, paler, and rounder, the size of saucers. There were other kinds, too, but she said they weren't good to eat.

"After the ceremony we'll pick the good ones," Doña Celestina said.

We followed her down the hill through a pine forest to a fireplace—a small ring of stones around an earthen floor.

"This is the place—Mundo's shrine," Doña Celestina said. "Many people have made offerings here."

We set down all we were carrying. J'aal looked to me to throw the ball again, but I shook my head and put it away.

Doña Celestina had told me earlier about the day 13 Q'anil. It was extremely powerful, she'd said—a day to celebrate beginnings and endings, to ask for the sprouting of new plants, or the harvest of ripe crops. To celebrate a birth. Or a death.

When she'd said "death," I'd been filled with dread. I thought the little red seeds had been telling her I was going to die. But she'd said that when the little seeds showed the date 13 Q'anil, that almost never meant physical death. It meant, instead, some great and necessary change coming about in one's life. 13 Q'anil was the strongest day to kill and bury weaknesses or any bad or evil things in oneself that needed to be got rid of. And it was the very best day to plant good things in oneself.

I should think about that, she'd said, when she performed the ceremony for me.

Doña Celestina knelt and kissed the rocks of the shrine. She opened her bundle and took out candles in many colors and stood them up against the rocks with their tips leaning together and meeting in the center of the ring.

She talked to the candles, asking them to feed the ancestors, the Ahau, and Mundo, and then she lit them.

We stood watching. Even J'aal, staring at the flames, seemed to know the fire was special. The candles burned fast, the colored wax melting into the earth. Doña Celestina tossed balls of copal into the flames, and thick black smoke and a rich spicy scent whirled up from the fire.

She gave me two ears of dry corn from her bundle. I passed them through the smoke, the way she told me, so their nourishment would rise to Mundo and the Ahau, and then I laid them on top of the fallen candles.

Doña Celestina circled the fire, chanting in Ixil. She told the Lord God she was just a servant of him, Mundo, and the ancestors. She told the day 13 Q'anil that everything was prepared, everything had been sown, and she was there to help bring the reaping to completion. She asked 13 Q'anil to give me a harvest, she asked Mundo, the Ahau, and Holy María of the Lilies also, to defend me, free me from Uncle, and help me find my parents. She asked them to remove all weaknesses from me, and all obstacles from my road.

I believed Doña Celestina and I thanked her for the ceremony, yet all the same I began to feel sad, and I didn't know why. Maybe because I couldn't feel any great change in myself. But I didn't want Doña Celestina to see my sadness, and so I smiled.

"Let's show Tzunún the two rivers," Doña Amalia said.

We left our things by the shrine. Below it, the land sloped down, covered by a net of exposed tree roots. Tall slender young trees grew from the net of roots, their branches thick with orchids and the strangling green vines we call tree-killers. But the young trees were still strong and alive.

We walked out from under the trees to a shallow, intensely green river with gentle rapids. Little streams from the hills on both sides fed into it.

"People have named this the river of joy," Doña Amalia said.

The day was hot, but the water was cool. We hitched up our skirts and waded, J'aal splashing beside us. Sandy circles of stone, white as salt and sharp to the touch, made a lacy pattern on the river bottom. Doña Celestina said dissolved stone in the water settled out to make the pattern, like dissolved sugar going to the bottom of a coffee cup.

We walked slowly downstream, catching on to each other's hands when we slipped. Even J'aal slipped; she braced herself on all four paws sometimes.

"Where's the other river?" I said.

Doña Celestina pointed to where it tumbled down from a mountain at the far end of the valley.

"The river of fear," Doña Amalia said.

"It comes from high up," Doña Celestina said, "and then it goes underground. We're walking over it. Nobody knows where it comes out, but we can go see where it enters the earth."

Only we never did that, because of a plant Doña Amalia saw growing right near us in the river of joy. She plucked a leaf and tasted it. Watercress, she said it was, and it would be good in a salad with our lunch.

She asked me to pick it while she and Doña Celestina went to harvest the mushrooms.

They were leaving when I saw a swirl of red floating in the water. Red the color of blood, coming from J'aal's paws.

"J'aal's bleeding!" I shouted.

Doña Celestina and Doña Amalia waded back to us. Doña Amalia lifted J'aal's front paws, first one, then the other. J'aal yelped.

"She's got cuts, poor thing."

"It's the white stone," Doña Celestina said, "the circles. We have sandals to protect our feet. J'aal doesn't."

"You come up to the waterfall with us, J'aal!" Doña Amalia said. "The ground is soft there."

Even though the rocks hurt her, J'aal didn't want to go. She looked toward the road and barked.

"Maybe there are sheep on the road," Doña Amalia said. "That's probably her temptation."

Doña Amalia and Doña Celestina waded off through the shallow water, calling J'aal to follow them. She didn't move.

"Go, J'aal! Go!" I told her.

She looked at me doubtfully.

"For your own sake, J'aal," I told her. "Go!"

She limped across the river, walking between Doña Celestina and Doña Amalia. They patted her head; then they entered the trees and I couldn't see them or J'aal anymore.

34

The Cave

Thin streaks of J'aal's blood paled in the water and vanished. Her cuts weren't deep, but I worried anyway and felt gloomy.

Was her blood in the water a sign? How could a person know when something was a sign and when it was just natural? Maybe even Doña Celestina didn't always know for sure.

I gathered the watercress stem by stem, looking around for signs—good ones, bad ones, even signs that I should stop looking for signs. There weren't any.

The sun sparkled like shooting stars on the green river. Beyond the river back toward the road, I saw a man come out of the trees—a flaco, a skinny guy in dark clothes. He put his hand to his forehead like a visor to shade his eyes, and scanned the valley.

He carried something over his shoulder. He didn't have a hat. Only crazy men go around without hats. He scared me.

I rolled the watercress up in my shawl. Even if I didn't have enough, I was leaving. I'd be safe from him up at the waterfall with my dog and my friends. I splashed in that direction through the shallow water.

The flaco started running along the river's edge. Before I could reach my friends, I'd meet him first. I stood in the water watching him, not sure what to do. He picked up a stone and threw it in my direction, and from his movements I knew the worst. I could never cross the river to my friends and be safe. The crazy flaco was Uncle.

The old snake demon bulged in my throat. Its enormous coils wrapped round my heart and crushed the air from my lungs. I opened my mouth to scream for Doña Celestina and Doña Amalia and J'aal. No sound came out.

I dropped my shawl and started wading to the far side of the river, away from my friends. Away from Uncle, too. As soon as I got to dry ground, I ran. I couldn't see a path, but I knew I had to keep going. I started up a rocky slope. Uncle was in the river, coming after me.

The rocky hill got steeper. I climbed as fast as I could, bushes and thorny plants catching at my clothes.

A white cliff blocked my path. There was no way to climb it. I ran alongside it, hearing stones tumbling down the hill behind me, Uncle scrambling in the rocks. Behind a thick mat of bushes, I saw a hollow in the cliff—a place where I could hide, I thought. I clawed my way through the bushes.

The hollow was the entrance to a cave. I crawled in.

After the bright sun outside, I was blinded by its darkness, but I kept going, groping my way along the cave wall. It was smooth and cool, and in just a few feet it curved, becoming a great pillar of rock. I lay down behind it and put my arms partway around it. It felt like a great tree, a great tree climbing to the top of the world.

In the silence I heard Uncle, kicking his way through the brush, hollering "Rosa!"

His voice got fainter, then was lost in the silence. He had passed by. I kissed the pillar of rock. Tears of gratitude ran down my cheeks. The cave had saved me, and not only the cave, but Mundo, its spirit. Doña Celestina had prayed for Mundo to protect me. Surely he was with me, taking care of me.

If I outwaited Uncle, I'd be free.

Behind the pillar the cave was totally dark, totally silent, yet I could sense the enormous weight of rock above it, below it, and on all sides. The entire Earth sheltered me. The god Mundo, so big he could crush anyone, didn't hurt me, he hugged me, he protected me. Maybe inside my mother, before I was born, I'd felt that safe when her whole body had hugged and fed and protected me. Now Mundo, all around me, was feeding me with his strength, and I was part of him.

I wanted to be with him forever and never be afraid.

Fear had been my whole life—fear of Uncle. Running to keep up with Uncle. Running to hide with Uncle when he did something bad. Moving my legs like a puppet. Being ordered—"Go here! Go there!" And now still hiding. Running from Uncle.

Being with Uncle, running from Uncle—it had never been a life. A life is something great.

A worm crawling in the ground had a better, nobler existence than Uncle. At least a worm is honest. Uncle wasn't. Maybe he'd come to make me leave with him. But I wouldn't go. I'd rather die than be his slave again.

Or maybe he'd come to kill me. If he found the cave, he might. But it didn't matter. There was a part of me he couldn't kill. I was in Mundo, and Mundo was in me.

I'd heard that people feel calm when they're about to die, that death doesn't frighten them at all; it's simply the next step into the unknown. Just like being born.

I felt calm and very clear, in danger, but not worried. I wondered if that meant that I would die soon. Probably it did. But first I'd see the cave. Mundo's place.

I remembered the flashlight Doña Amalia had given me. I took it from around my neck and turned it on.

35

The Ancestor

I walked deeper into the cave. The flashlight made a little circle of white on the rock around me, fluttering upward like a butterfly to the great vault of the cave roof, and then on to the far wall, so far off it hardly showed at all in the thin beam of light.

The ground slanted downward, whitish and scattered with small pebbles. I came to the back wall, which had a tall narrow opening to a farther room. I shone my light into it, but I could see nothing. From it, like a warning not to go on, a black wind whirled by me, and I cried out. I'd awakened bats in the next chamber. Terrified, they flew past me, out into the light of day.

I moved away from the passage and lit the other side of the first chamber. The little circle of light zigzagged, exposed glassy rocks like melting candles that dripped from high up.

I rested against the wall of the chamber and felt a fine-edged line of rock against my back. I shone my light on it and saw a niche that had been carved into the rock. It was covered with a thick layer of glassy black stones that made a bed, and on the bed was a skeleton.

He was all delicate white bones. Arm bones and rib bones, leg bones and all the tiny bones that form feet. A few scraps of faded cloth that must have been his clothes lay around him. Scattered among his ribs and the loose bones of his hands were black beads that must have been a necklace.

His skull was mostly hidden under a mask of green stone, with stone eyes bluer than the sky that looked toward the mouth of the cave and the world of light.

The lips of the mask were gently smiling. I touched them. They were smooth as water.

Above the forehead, the mask took on the shape of a bird—a bird with a fine, narrow beak and outspread wings. I caught my breath. It was a colibrí. The bird that I was named for.

A hummingbird is fearless. If it must, it will fight something a thousand times bigger than it. And people say that when the bravest ancestors died in battle, their spirits flew to the next world, and they are still in that world, immortal hummingbirds.

I touched the stone wings, the beak, the eyes. I touched

the hand of the ancestor, his clean and simple bones. I was not scared, not the way I had been in the cemetery in San Sebastián among the tombs. The ancestor was not restless. He had been dead many hundreds of years. He didn't want to hurt anyone, I could tell that. His spirit had flown. In another world he dipped nectar from immortal flowers. He was at peace.

Soon I would be with him. He had left behind a treasure, the treasure I'd been supposed to find for so many years. The prophecies were all but fulfilled. All that was missing was for Uncle to come back.

Near the entrance to the cave, I turned out my light and lay down again, clinging to my pillar of stone. I told myself I was making sure that Uncle was gone before I went to Doña Celestina. But deep in my heart, I knew I was waiting for Uncle.

Air vibrated all around me with the press of wings, then fell still. The bats had returned to their world of darkness.

Maybe hours had passed since I'd glimpsed Uncle. Or maybe only minutes. Or maybe days, weeks, eternities.

Outside the cave, bushes rustled. I heard his voice, hoarse, cracked, triumphant.

"Bats! I saw bats! Flying here! To this cave! They don't come out by day unless someone bothers them! I know where you are, Rosa! I've—*got you!*"

36

I Couldn't Stop Listening

I could hear Uncle's breathing. I could feel him looking, listening, peering into the cave. I could smell him, and he stank.

But he didn't know for sure I was there, not really. He couldn't know where I was in all that darkness. But he wanted me to hear him, so he shouted into it, his voice echoing around me. He was going to tell me everything, he said, and most of all, what he thought of me, Rosa Soplona, Rosa the snitch, Rosa the traitor.

I willed myself not to hear. If I could've done it, that would've saved me. But my will wasn't strong enough. I heard every word.

I'd ruined his life, he said. How he and Raimundo had suffered in the big city jail where there wasn't enough food to eat! The only reason they'd survived was that the police let them and other prisoners wash cars on the street. Under guard, of course. That way they'd earned a few quetzales to spend on food. They got to keep their own clothes, too, because there were no uniforms.

Just before their trial, they'd escaped, busted out of an exercise terrace on the roof. With money and their own clothes, they thought they'd make it. They ran over the rooftops till the cops started shooting. Uncle had made it, but Raimundo was dead. Because of me, Uncle said. Really I was the one who had killed his best friend.

He'd fooled the sheep that were Doña Celestina's neighbors. When he got to Nebaj, he didn't ask for me. He just asked where the Day-Keeper was and said he wanted a ceremony. Well, she's at Two Rivers, they said. But he'd found me, not her.

So she was still alive, I thought. And that meant Doña Amalia was alive, too, and J'aal. Maybe they were looking for me.

He said he didn't want to see the Day-Keeper anyhow, he'd already seen enough of that witch. He'd lied and he'd fooled her when he said he hadn't been at La Hortensia. He'd seen her afterward, too—only for a second from the army truck, but he'd always remembered her. Because of her eyes.

His voice shifted and I knew that something really bad was coming. I covered my ears with my hands, but he shouted louder than ever, and the sound went right through me.

"Her eyes were just like your mother's, Rosa, the day that I took you. —Yes, Rosa, it was me. I took you, took you, took you from your mother!

"Stop screaming! You won't? Well, no matter—I've got you now, stop screaming."

37

River of Fear

He pulled me out into the light and held me tight by the hair. He had a coil of rope around his shoulder.

"I like rope," he said. He tied it around my waist and tied my hands behind my back. He held the rope in his fist and stepped back and looked at me, and his look told me that I would die.

He would kill me right off, he said, except that he wondered about the treasure. He figured I must have found it by now if I was ever going to find it. But if I hadn't, he would kill me anyhow, because he was sick of waiting for it. But, he said, with his bloodshot eyes gleaming, if I showed him the treasure, he'd forgive me for everything, and we could go on the road again.

I thought, *I'll never tell you about the treasure, no matter what.* Not because of the ancestor, who didn't need it anymore. Because I wouldn't dirty myself or my life. I wouldn't steal for Uncle or hide for Uncle, or run with Uncle or run from Uncle, ever again. I wasn't going on the road with Uncle, not ever. I had my own road. It was short, but it was shining, and when it ended, I would be a hummingbird.

I wouldn't fight Uncle with my body. Not because I was afraid; I just couldn't stand contact with him. Still, I wouldn't submit. He could kill me, but he couldn't defeat me. I was part of Mundo, I could still feel that, and like a warrior I would have a great life till the instant I died.

"So where's the treasure?" Uncle said.

I didn't answer. I thought he'd finish me for that, but he just chuckled. "Always were a quiet one." Maybe he thought I was too terrified to talk.

He stood watching me, trying to read my eyes. And then he guessed. "It's here, isn't it?" I didn't answer. He took the flashlight from me and pushed me ahead of him into the cave.

He shone the light all around, not where I needed it to see. I stumbled in the darkness, but the rope held me up. We got to the niche and the shining bed of stones where the ancestor was lying.

Uncle flashed the light on the bones and the mask, and he laughed. He said the mask was just stone and it was worthless.

He stood sucking air in through the gaps in his teeth.

He moved the mask and stuck his fingers through the eye sockets of the skull and lifted it. Underneath, there were tiny figures of jaguars carved in gold.

"I have it now!" Uncle said. "I have it forever!" He dumped the gold into his pockets and pushed me ahead of him out of the cave.

"Certainly there's more treasure here, deeper in," Uncle gloated. "Enough for a lifetime. I'll come back for it! I can get it anytime!"

He couldn't if I lived. I'd squeal on him again. He had to know that.

He tightened the knots in the rope that went around me. "I owe you a little piece of paper," he said. He laughed. "I'll give you that at the river."

We got down the hill to the shallow river. If he handed something over there, maybe I could trip him, make him slip on the stone circles. Hold him down.

"This is the wrong river," he said. He made me walk ahead. I had no chance to trip him.

We waded through the river of joy, then up onto dry rock. I couldn't see the river of fear, but I could hear it.

And then we were on the cliff above it, looking far down to where it thundered and roared, spewing foam, and it was a terrible thing to see.

Big boulders it had pulled out of the mountainside higher up tumbled and bounced like pebbles in its current. Tree trunks it had torn loose swirled and collided. And then, suddenly, sucking everything it carried, it plunged into a dark tunnel in the rock, and disappeared underground. Down deep under the river of joy, it was still flowing, still roaring. No one could see it. No one could hear it. But it was there. Whoever fell into it aboveground would never come out.

" 'Mundo said to cut off your tongue and your ears," Uncle told me. "I won't do that." As if he were offering me a treat.

Uncle took his old wallet out of his pocket. "Your paper's here. Do you want it?"

He let out a few feet more of the rope he had coiled around his shoulder. I moved as far away from him as I could, in the direction of the distant mountains.

"Say you want it. Say, 'Please, Uncle!' and I'll give it to you."

I didn't care what he offered or what he had, I wouldn't answer him. I wouldn't touch anything of his. I would never speak.

He made a face and tossed the wallet toward me.

"Don't talk, then," he said. "Just go get it. I want you to have it. I want to see it in your hands."

Doña Celestina had told me I had to get the paper. But now, when I had the chance, I knew I shouldn't take it. Something about the way Uncle was standing told me that. Told me maybe there wasn't a paper. Told me even if there was, I wouldn't see it long.

"I owe it to you. I give it to you," Uncle said. He

smiled. He held out his right hand, palm up, like a man hiding nothing. His left hand tightened on the rope.

His eyes glittered. He looked like a jaguar about to spring.

I wouldn't reach for his wallet, that's what I decided. I wouldn't give him that satisfaction.

"I'll untie your hands," Uncle said. "I'll make it easy."

He tied my legs together. He freed my hands, pinning them between one arm and his knee while he did it. He let out more of the rope around my waist and went back to the cliff's edge, where he stood watching me.

"You can get it now, easy," Uncle said. "Soon as you have it, then I'll let you go."

Once I had the wallet in my hand, that's when he would do it. That's when he'd pull me to him and throw me in the river, in with the tree trunks and the boulders and the current that would take me underneath the earth forever.

"Truly," Uncle said. "Truly, once you have it, then I'll let you go."

He sounded so sincere. Part of me believed him.

The wallet was between us. I hobbled toward it. Closer to him. Closer to the river of fear.

I stood over the wallet.

"Pick it up!" Uncle said.

I bent down and picked up a rock. I threw it as hard as I could. It hit him in the chest and he cursed. "To the devil with the paper!" he said. "To the devil with you!" He started hauling on the rope, pulling me closer and closer. To him. To the cliff. To the river of fear.

I took tiny steps to keep from falling. That made it easier for him, too. He stared at me, smiling.

He thought he was controlling me, but inside myself I commanded him with all the power of my thought: *Look at me until the end.*

And he did. Maybe he hoped to see the pain in my eyes, but I wouldn't show it. Maybe he hoped to see fear. I wouldn't show it. Nor hope, either. I only showed that I saw him.

I never took my gaze off his. He never took his eyes off me. Inside myself I commanded him not to turn his head, and he didn't. He never saw J'aal till she growled deep in her chest, and by then she was up on her hind legs, going for his throat. He raised his arms against her and dropped the rope, but his arms couldn't stop her and her teeth slashed his neck. He stumbled backward, his arms flailing, with J'aal on top of him. He was going over the cliff into the river, and J'aal was going, too.

I sprang. I leaped. I turned in the air. Something snapped in my ankle when I tackled her, but I didn't go over.

Neither did she.

38

A Little Piece of Paper

Doña Celestina and Doña Amalia caressed my hair and made me sit up. Doña Amalia noticed my broken ankle. She felt the bone and put it back together right. I screamed while she moved it, but I managed not to cry while she bound it with a cloth and a straight stick.

After that I started shaking. Not just my head, my whole body.

"It's shock," Doña Amalia said. "You've had a fright."

It wasn't shock. It was just that my mind was gone, lost to the swirling river beneath the earth.

They wrapped me in their shawls. They rubbed my hands, my arms, my back, until my mind came back into my body. I stared around as if I were seeing the world for the first time.

Doña Amalia pointed. "What's that lying on the rock?"

"Uncle's wallet," I said. "He offered it to me. He said the little paper he owed me is in it. But I don't want it. I don't care what's in it!"

Doña Celestina picked up the wallet and opened it. It was empty.

"He lied," I said.

Doña Celestina nodded but said nothing. It seemed she was listening to a voice in the wind. An ancestor talking to her about the wallet in her hand.

She tugged at it until its worn stitches broke. A small paper fell from it and landed on the rocks.

A breeze took it. Doña Amalia scrambled to her feet and caught it right at the edge of the cliff and brought it back to me.

I unfolded it, a pale square no bigger than my hand, with four tiny pinholes in the corners. Once it had been pinned inside clothing, fastened by a mother inside a child's huipil.

The paper was damp, but the ink had held firm, firm as the hand that had once written on it in clear blue letters, softly rounded.

This child is:
Tzunún Chumil
75, Calle del Calvario
San Juan Sacatepequez

39

The Reunion

I never told anybody, even Doña Celestina, about the treasure or about becoming one with Mundo in the cave. Maybe, one day, I will. And maybe one day I'll find that, somehow, Doña Celestina already knows. But right now I don't want to risk what I feel: Mundo is part of me.

At first I couldn't think very well, at least the kind of normal thinking that people do every day. I hadn't learned to use my crutches very well, either, with only one day of practice.

Doña Celestina and Doña Amalia had set my narrow bed out on the patio. J'aal lay by my side.

I had new ribbons wound into my hair. On the cast the doctor had put on my leg, Doña Celestina and Doña Amalia had made drawings—suns, and moons, and the planet Earth. Hummingbirds and stars.

My ankle hurt, but otherwise I was all right. In my mind I could still see my shining road. I didn't know where it was going exactly, but I knew it was good and would stretch a long way.

At moments I was scared my parents wouldn't really want me. Then I thought that at least they should. I was more worried about J'aal. Maybe my parents wouldn't let me keep her: I knew they were honest people, and J'aal was a stolen dog.

Doña Celestina read the seeds about that. She said yes, my parents would search for the first owner of J'aal, because of how they'd suffered missing me. They wouldn't want to steal a living being from anyone. I asked her if they'd find J'aal's real owner, and she said yes—but only a person with a heart of stone would take J'aal from me, and the seeds said J'aal's owner didn't have a heart of stone.

So I hoped for the best.

When the bell rang, Doña Amalia went to the gate. Doña Celestina stayed with me and held my hand.

Just when I should have been happiest, my heart burst with sadness. "Doña Celestina," I whispered, "I wish you were my mother."

She squeezed my hand. "You'll come to visit me," she said. "We'll be friends. Always, always."

J'aal sat up, her ears cocked, listening.

A man and woman walked toward me. They smiled. My mother. My father. I remembered them young—but they weren't young anymore. Deep lines were etched into their faces.

Doña Celestina helped me stand up. I put my arm around her and took a step toward them. One step to span so many years, to cross eternities of grief.

My parents opened their arms to me. Doña Celestina released me, and my father held me up.

His voice rumbled softly against my ear. My mother kissed my face, my hair. Her hands slid warm along my arms. "Tzunún!" she cried. "My child! My darling Colibrí!"

I still knew them. I felt as if they'd just waked me from a dream, as if I'd been asleep a thousand years.

We held each other till the strangeness left us, and for a little while we melted into one—one family shining like the sun, brighter than the universe of stars.

ACKNOWLEDGMENTS

I wish to thank: Tereso Joj, Administrative Director of the Mayan university, Universidad del Valle, Guatemala Altiplano; Arnulfo Axpuac, Mayan priest; Cayetana Xicay Esquít, midwife; María del Carmen Tui, diviner; Luis Queché, herbal healer and diviner; Richard N. Adams and David Libbey, anthropologists; Michael Shawcross, caver; Dr. Hugo René Sicán, veterinarian; Fernando Quezada Toruño and José Aguilar, lawyers; Dr. Gove Hambidge, psychiatrist, as well as Miguel and Elisa Cacrúm, Margarita and Isabela Par, Manuel Morales, Blanca Esthela Cúmes Chopén, and Rosa Queché Can for being my consultants in the creation of *Colibrí*.